ALMOST Perfection

LYNN LAFLEUR

Ellora's Cave
Romantica Publishing

What the critics are saying...

5 Stars "Lynn Lafleur is a brilliant author. Her stories are captivating and sensual with a flare for the dramatic. Almost Perfection is a five star masterpiece that will leave any reader wanting more. I can not wait to read whatever she writes next and I can only hope she has more in store for her Cooper's Companions series." ~ *Sensual Ecata Romance*

An Ellora's Cave Romantica Publication

www.ellorascave.com

Almost Perfection

ISBN 9781419959363
ALL RIGHTS RESERVED.
Almost Perfection Copyright © 2009 Lynn LaFleur
Edited by Raelene Gorlinsky.
Photography and cover art by Les Byerley.

This book printed in the U.S.A. by Jasmine-Jade Enterprises, LLC.

Electronic book Publication March 2009
Trade paperback Publication August 2009

With the exception of quotes used in reviews, this book may not be reproduced or used in whole or in part by any means existing without written permission from the publisher, Ellora's Cave Publishing, Inc.® 1056 Home Avenue, Akron OH 44310-3502.

Warning: The unauthorized reproduction or distribution of this copyrighted work is illegal. Criminal copyright infringement, including infringement without monetary gain, is investigated by the FBI and is punishable by up to 5 years in federal prison and a fine of $250,000.
(http://www.fbi.gov/ipr/)

This book is a work of fiction and any resemblance to persons, living or dead, or places, events or locales is purely coincidental. The characters are productions of the author's imagination and used fictitiously.

ALMOST PERFECTION

Trademarks Acknowledgement

ಬ

The author acknowledges the trademarked status and trademark owners of the following wordmarks mentioned in this work of fiction:

Coke: The Coca-Cola Company Corporation

Dallas Cowboys: Dallas Cowboys Football Club, Ltd.

Dallas Mavericks: Radical Mavericks Management, LLC

Indiana Pacers: Pacers Basketball Corporation

Miss America: The Miss America Organization

Star-Telegram: *Fort Worth Star-Telegram*, The McClatchy Company

Chapter One

๛

Brent Cooper flopped down in one of the chairs before his sister's desk and glared at her. She'd become immune to his glares a long time ago, but he tried one anyway. She stared right back at him, her expression calm.

"It won't hurt you to help me, Brent."

"I don't think this is necessary."

Michelle clasped her hands together and rested them on the desk. Brent braced himself for the upcoming lecture. His sister was very good at lectures. "There are thousands of women in the Metroplex who might need an escort and would use Coopers' Companions if they knew more about us."

"We advertise in the phone book and newspaper. The proof of our big Christmas ad is on your desk. Our guys are busy almost every weekend, so our ads are working."

"They aren't working well enough. We need a presence on the web. Professional women are busy. They don't take the time to read the newspaper or look in phone books. When they want information, they do a search on the internet. I set up a website a couple of years ago, but it's outdated and boring. We need a fresh look. I want pictures and descriptions of the guys. I want a woman to drool when she clicks on Reese's or Daryl's picture."

"Or mine," he said with a grin.

Michelle rolled her eyes. "You are so full of yourself."

He shrugged. "I have eyes. I know what I see when I look in a mirror."

Brent had never believed in false modesty. All three Cooper children had been blessed with exceptional good looks, especially his older brother Zach. He'd been the star of Coopers' Companions until he'd met Jade Talmage and officially retired as an escort. They'd married two months ago.

Now Brent was the star. He had his choice of the prettiest women with the best bodies. He liked it at the top and planned to stay there.

Propping his ankle on the opposite knee, he linked his hands over his stomach. "So tell me about this Robin…whatever her last name is."

"Robin Howell. Jade recommended her. She just revamped the hospital's site. Jade said Robin did a great job."

"So she works in front of a computer all day. Her ass is probably as wide as our front door."

"Sheesh, you are such a jerk. What difference does it make how she looks?"

"I know what I like. What's wrong with that?"

She gave him a look that clearly said she didn't agree with his thinking. Too bad. Brent enjoyed beautiful women and wasn't ashamed of that fact.

The bell over the front door rang, announcing someone had come in. "That's probably Robin." Michelle stood and pointed a finger at him. "Be nice."

"Yes, ma'am."

He could hear the two women talking in the foyer, but couldn't make out their words. Not that he cared. He was only here because Michelle threatened his life if he didn't cooperate.

He chuckled. He loved to pick on his baby sister. Correction—*younger* sister. She quickly corrected him every time he treated her as a girl instead of a woman. She'd be twenty-seven in less than three weeks. He clearly remembered the ten-year-old brat who followed her brothers everywhere they went and made them miserable.

It was really hard for him to realize his little sister had grown up into such a lovely woman.

"Robin, this is my brother, Brent."

He looked up, and felt as if he'd been tackled by the Dallas Cowboys defensive line. Robin Howell didn't look at all as he'd imagined. Golden blonde hair was held in place on top of her head in one of those funny-looking clips like Michelle used. Various shades of blonde flowed through her hair, not the single color of a dye job. He knew women could get that streaky look from a hairdresser. He'd bet next week's paycheck that Robin's was natural.

Hazel eyes were surrounded by long eyelashes thickened with mascara. She had an ivory complexion that probably tanned easily. Full lips, high cheekbones, a long neck, voluptuous body. She was an incredibly attractive woman.

Exactly his type.

Her eyes held the deer-in-the-headlights look. He loved having such a strong effect on women. He slowly rose from his chair, a welcoming smile on his lips.

She blinked her eyes and straightened her shoulders. After clearing her throat, she held out her hand to him. "Nice to meet you, Brent."

Lifting her hand to his mouth, he kissed the back. "Hi, Robin. I'm very pleased to meet you."

Michelle rolled her eyes again. "Don't mind him, Robin. Brent thinks all women find him irresistible."

"Only the ones with good taste."

Robin tugged her hand away from his. "Are you one of the escorts, Brent?"

"Yes, I am. Want to hire me?"

Huffing out an irritated breath, Michelle slapped him on the arm. "Behave. I don't want you scaring Robin off before we even get started. Why don't you make us some coffee or hot tea?"

"Which do you prefer, Robin?" Brent asked.

"Hot tea would be nice."

He flashed her his friendliest smile. "Coming right up."

* * * * *

Brent Cooper had been born to charm women.

It had taken Robin Howell less than one minute in the same room with Michelle Cooper's brother to make that determination. Tall, with a swimmer's broad-shouldered build, the handsome blue-eyed blond oozed sex appeal.

He made her think of walking sin.

Her stomach had clenched at the first sight of him, a natural reaction to seeing a man so attractive. His cocky grin and phony charm quickly squelched any desire. She'd dealt with a handsome, conceited man in the past. She didn't want to ever deal with another one.

"My sister-in-law Jade said you did a wonderful job for the hospital. She was very pleased."

Michelle's comment dragged Robin away from thoughts of the past and back to the present. "Jade was easy to work with. She gave me an idea of what she wanted and let me create."

"That's what I want too." Michelle sat behind the desk and motioned for Robin to take the chair next to her. "I have some ideas, but I want you to work your magic."

Robin removed her laptop from the leather case and set it on the desk. "I like to work with my clients and create the exact look they want. I'll show you how to make changes and upload them yourself should you choose to do so instead of my doing them."

"I'm good with numbers and flowers. I'm not so great with graphics. The website I created two years ago is way outdated."

Robin smiled. She liked Michelle's honesty. "You don't have to be great with graphics. I'll do all the hard, time-consuming stuff for you." She pulled a legal pad from a pocket in her case, along with a file folder containing her pricing information. "Here's a list of my costs. Naturally, the more you want on your website, the more it will cost. But I promise all my clients a twenty-four-hour turnaround. Once I design and upload your site, any changes you want will be completed in one day."

"Sounds good."

Brent came back in the room carrying a tray with three mugs of hot tea. Robin watched him set the tray on the desk. He winked at her before picking up one mug and returning to his chair.

He studied her as he sipped his tea. Robin could almost *feel* his gaze moving over her hair, her eyes, her mouth, and down to her breasts...checking her out as if she would be his latest conquest.

Fat chance of that *happening.*

Robin faced Michelle again. "We'll need a photographer to take pictures of your escorts."

"Nathan can take the pictures." A dreamy smile crossed Michelle's lips. "He's wonderful."

That dreamy smile told Robin that this Nathan was far more than an employee to Michelle. She made a note on her pad—*have photographer.* "We'll need to set up a time or times for the guys to come in." She looked around the spacious, comfortable office. "We could set up in here. There should be plenty of room."

"What about some outside shots?" Michelle asked. "The backyard still has flowers blooming."

"I doubt if our guys want to be photographed surrounded by flowers," Brent said, his lips curving in a smirking grin.

Michelle stuck her tongue out at him.

Robin lowered her chin so they wouldn't see her grin. Obviously Michelle could hold her own against her brother.

Once more composed, she looked at Michelle again. "I think the inside shots will be fine. It's still warm outdoors, but it's supposed to turn cold by Wednesday." She made another note on her pad—*inside photos*. "Does Nathan have back drapes or should I pick them up?"

"He has a black one and a silver one. I'm not sure about other colors."

"I'm thinking about making the background on your site either black or dark gray. I'd rather use a different drape than black. Maybe jewel tones depending on the escort's hair and skin color."

Michelle smiled. "I like that idea."

"What about black and white photos?" Brent asked.

Robin looked at Brent. He'd made a good suggestion. People often used black and white photos instead of full color on their sites.

Perhaps there was a brain behind that smirk after all.

"It's up to you and Michelle. I'll go whichever way you want. We can take both and see which ones you prefer."

Michelle nodded. "Let's do that. I'll talk to Nathan tonight about taking the pictures and see if he has any drapes."

Robin added *check on drapes* to her growing list. "Now, time of the pictures. Will your guys be able to come during the day or would evening be better?"

"Probably evening. Most of them have regular daytime jobs."

"When do you want me to start on your site?"

"Now."

Brent laughed. "My sister isn't the most patient person in the world, Robin."

A blush colored Michelle's cheeks. "I'm sorry. Would you rather wait until after Thanksgiving?"

"I'd be happy to start now. That'll give me the chance to work on it over the Thanksgiving holiday weekend. I have several design examples on my laptop. You can pick the one you like best, or I'll design something different if none of those please you."

"Chelle, you want me to email the guys about the pictures? I can do that so you and Robin can get started on whatever she wants to show you."

"That would be great. Thanks."

"I'll cover the phones. Why don't you and Robin go back to your office so you won't be bothered?"

Propping her elbows on the desk, Michelle held her own mug of tea in both hands. "Who are you and what have you done with my brother?"

Brent scowled. "Ha ha."

Her eyes twinkled with laughter over the rim of her mug as she sipped her tea. "I appreciate your offer." She set her mug on the desk. "Maybe some of the guys could stop by tomorrow evening so we can start on the pictures."

"Don't you need to talk to Nathan first?" Brent asked.

Michelle shook her head. "I'm sure he'll be fine with it. He doesn't have any plans until Thursday morning when he and Andre pick up Andre's brother at the airport." She turned to Robin. "Can you be here tomorrow evening?"

"No problem."

"We can split the guys into two groups—fifteen one night, fourteen one night. Or I guess fifteen both nights, since Brent is an escort."

Robin glanced at Brent. He would love to know what she was thinking. Perhaps she wondered how he'd be as an escort...and a lover.

He was excellent at both. He charmed a woman thoroughly while escorting her. More often than not, the evening ended in her bed. Never in his bed. He didn't believe in taking a woman home with him. He liked to give her pleasure, then go home alone. No awkward morning afters, no promises of seeing her again. It was a job and he made sure every woman knew that.

Both his siblings had fallen in love. That was fine for them. Brent was happy with his single life and planned to keep everything the same. He enjoyed fucking a different woman every week and saw no reason to give up his freedom.

"I'll want pictures of you and your brothers for the information page about the business," Robin said.

"Sure. Brent, will you call Zach and ask him to come by tomorrow evening?"

"I talked to him this morning. He'll be here this afternoon."

"Great." She turned back to Robin. "Since Brent is willing to watch the phones, we can go back to my office and get started."

"Okay."

Robin looked at him again as she closed her laptop. The woman was definitely interested. Brent wondered how long he should wait to ask her out.

He'd escorted a woman to a company winging last weekend. She'd been in her early fifties and looked like she ate donuts for breakfast every morning. Brent had breathed a sigh of relief when she'd tipped him generously at her front door and said goodnight. Although it was always up to the escort if the evening continued after the social event, Brent would have performed as always if she'd shown any interest in sex, even though he would rather fuck a young, attractive woman.

Like Robin.

She wore a long-sleeved ivory jacket over a matching T-shirt. The shirt snuggled her full breasts. He guessed she wore at least a D cup. He was rarely wrong when it came to women's breasts.

The two women gathered up Robin's paperwork and laptop. He admired the gentle sway of Robin's hips in her brown slacks as she walked out of the room. She did have a mighty fine ass. He could hardly wait to grip it while he sank his cock into her wet pussy.

He pressed his hand to his burgeoning hard-on. Soon. He had no doubt he'd have her soon.

Chapter Two

Barely half an hour passed before Michelle jumped up from her chair and ran into the bathroom. Robin had noticed Michelle's face getting paler by the minute. She'd mentioned earlier that she'd tried a new recipe last night and it hadn't agreed with her. Something more than simply a bad recipe must be wrong.

Michelle opened the bathroom door and leaned against the frame. Her face was white, her eyes sunken and listless. Robin rose from her chair and hurried to Michelle's side, clasping her arm to help her stand. "Are you okay?"

"I don't think this is from my meatloaf."

"I don't either. Why don't you go home?"

Michelle waved a weak hand toward her desk. "What about the website?"

"You've given me a good idea of what you want. That's enough for me to start."

"Okay." She grimaced and pressed her hand to her stomach. "I'm sorry."

"Don't apologize for being sick. Go home and take care of yourself."

"Thanks, Robin. I'll tell Brent I'm leaving."

After Michelle left the room, Robin began gathering up her paperwork. She'd made several notes of what Michelle had in mind for Coopers' Companions' site, enough so she could begin working on it as soon as she got home.

"What are you doing?"

Robin looked up at the sound of Brent's voice. He stood in the doorway, casually leaning against the frame with his arms crossed over his chest. She wondered how long he'd stood there, watching her. "I'm getting my stuff together so I can go home."

"Why? Michelle said you need my help with the guys' info."

"I can start working on the site's layout without bothering you."

"You won't bother me." Grabbing the chair at the end of Michelle's desk, he moved it next to Robin and straddled it. "So, what do you need to know?"

His eyes were such an amazing blue, a cross between the sky and the ocean. Robin had noticed Michelle possessed the same eye color. Looking into Michelle's eyes didn't make her heart flutter the way it did when she looked into Brent's.

She didn't want anything to flutter around Brent. He was arrogant and egotistical and much too handsome to trust.

She had to get away from him.

"I don't want to hold you up if you have something to do—"

"My job is to be here in the office. As long as I have to be here, I can help you."

He sat close to her, close enough that she could easily reach out to him. He crossed his arms over the back of his chair. Robin imagined touching his hand, letting her fingers slowly travel up his arm. She would run them over his shoulder, his neck. She'd touch his thick mustache with one fingertip and find out if it was soft or coarse.

A delicious heat began to build low in her belly. It had been so long since she'd touched a man, so long since a man had touched her. She'd had a hot, passionate love affair once. She knew how it felt to desire a man, to feel those deep yearnings for his touch. The man was gone, but sometimes her yearnings were difficult to ignore.

She had no choice. She couldn't take the chance.

"I sent the email to all our escorts about the pictures," Brent said. "Several are checked out for the Thanksgiving holiday. We'll probably have to do some of the pictures after the long weekend."

Since he'd set things in motion with his escorts, Robin decided it would be rude to leave. Just because certain body parts fluttered around Brent didn't mean she had to pay attention to them. She'd do her job and get away from him as quickly as possible.

"I have plenty to do with the basic website before I add the pictures." She pulled her legal pad back out of her case. "Did Michelle tell you what information she wants on the site? I assume names and a brief description of the escorts' likes and dislikes."

Brent nodded. "Sounds good."

Robin made a note on her pad. "Do you have different fees for your escorts and do you want them listed?"

"We do have different fees, based on how long someone has been with us and customers' comments. Happy customers mean the escort earns more. Reese Barringer earns the most per hour. He's been with us eight years and is very popular." Frowning slightly, Brent rubbed one finger over his mustache. "I don't think I want individual fees on the website. I don't want a woman picking an escort based on how much she has to pay him instead of their compatibility. We do our best to match up the woman with an escort who has the same interests she does. If they spend an evening together, they should be able to talk to each other. Some of those social functions get pretty boring."

Robin agreed with that. She'd been to functions in the past when she had to concentrate to keep from yawning. "What about a range of fees?"

Brent remained silent for a moment as he rubbed his mustache. Robin assumed he did that when he was deep in thought. "Our fees begin at three hundred per hour. You can list that."

Three hundred dollars to have a handsome man on a woman's arm for an hour. Or in her bed. Robin didn't for a moment believe that the men from Coopers' Companions always said goodnight at their dates' front doors.

She wrote down the price. It didn't matter to her whether or not the escorts took the evening further than a simple social function. She certainly had no plans to hire one.

"Do women ever request a particular escort?"

Brent nodded. "All the time. They may have hired one in the past, or a friend recommended one of them. In fact, that's how Zach met Jade. Jade's daughter, Breanna, heard about Zach from a former date and specifically asked for him to escort Jade to an anniversary dinner at Jade's hospital." He chuckled. "He was a goner after the first date."

Robin smiled. She really liked Jade. It had been a pleasure to work with her on the hospital's website. "Do you get along with your sister-in-law?"

"Sure. Jade's the best. I'll admit I wasn't thrilled with their relationship at first. I didn't want Zach to leave the business. But he was adamant he wanted Jade and only Jade." He shrugged. "I couldn't get him to change his mind."

"Why would you even try?"

"Because he was our most requested escort. He had a reputation for charming the ladies within minutes of their meeting him. So now it's up to me to be the charming escort."

He flashed her a smile, which she guessed was supposed to make her fall at his feet. Instead, she caught herself before she rolled her eyes. "You told me Reese Barringer earns the most per hour."

"He does, of the hired escorts. I'm the top earner in the company."

She could hear the arrogance in his voice. "And you're proud of that."

His eyes turned sultry. "I do my job *very* well."

If she said "let's fuck", he'd be on top of her in a second. Robin had only met one other man in her life who was so sure of himself and his sexual appeal to women.

Her past experience was an excellent reason to stay away from Brent Cooper.

Sunlight flowed through the two large windows, warming the room as the minutes passed. The combination of the natural heat and Brent's nearness soon made Robin uncomfortable. She slipped off her jersey jacket and let it fall to the back of the chair behind her. Brent's gaze snapped to her upper arms. The cocky, self-assured look disappeared from his eyes. His lips tightened in a frown.

She was used to people's negative reaction when they saw the scars on her arms. The automatic disdain had hurt her at first. Over time, she'd learned to ignore it. She'd decided it wasn't her problem that people were so hung up over perfection that they would judge her based on her discolored skin. That's when she'd stopped hiding her arms and went back to wearing comfortable clothing, including sleeveless tops, instead of always wearing long sleeves.

"Not very pretty, are they?" Robin asked.

"What happened?"

"I was in a fire."

He lowered his gaze, as if he couldn't stand to look at her any longer. She normally ignored people's attitudes, but Brent's rankled her. He'd been flirting outrageously since she'd arrived. Now he wouldn't look her in the eyes.

"The scars on my back are much worse."

His gaze whipped to her face. His mouth tightened even more as he narrowed his eyes.

"Skin grafts and surgeries can only do so much with burns. The scars never completely go away."

Robin heard a bell, the same sound she'd heard when she'd entered Coopers' Companions. Brent stared at her another moment before he stood. "Excuse me," he muttered.

She watched him leave the office. He didn't look at her again.

Robin sighed and returned to her laptop. She needed to concentrate on the website instead of Brent Cooper's attitude.

Muted male voices became louder as they approached the office. She looked up when Brent stepped back into the room, followed by a handsome dark-haired man.

"Zach, this is Robin Howell, the woman Michelle hired to do our website. Robin, my brother Zach."

Zach gave her a friendly smile. "Hi, Robin."

His smile seemed sincere, not the same "come on" as Brent's. Zach's dark brown hair brushed his shoulders. His tanned skin made his blue eyes even more vivid. Jade was a very lucky lady to have such a hunk as her husband. "It's nice to meet you, Zach."

"Jade raved about your design talent. I'm glad you'll be working for us."

"Thank you."

Zach turned toward Brent. "You have the ad proof?"

"Yeah, in the office."

"Excuse us, Robin," Zach said, once more giving her a smile.

"Certainly."

Brent flashed a quick glance at her before following Zach from the room. His eyes no longer held the teasing, cocky look they had before he saw her scars.

It hurt, and that made her angry at herself. If he didn't like looking at her scars, he could stay away from her...the farther, the better.

* * * * *

Brent found the proof of the *Star-Telegram* ad buried beneath Michelle's pile of papers on the desk. It would help if Michelle filed more than once a year. He turned the legal-sized sheet so Zach could see it.

Zach sat in one of the leather chairs before the desk and studied the ad. "I like it." He looked up from the ad as Brent took the chair beside him. "What's the plan?"

"It'll run as a full page this Sunday and every Sunday until Christmas."

"Color or black and white?"

"Color. I want it to jump out at every single woman in the Metroplex."

"Michelle told me the Friday and Saturday before Christmas are already completely booked."

"They are. Wednesday and Thursday are filling up fast too. Lots of Christmas parties that week."

"Good." Zach laid the ad back on the desk, then looked directly into Brent's eyes. "What's up with you and Robin?"

Hiding anything from his brother was almost impossible. Zach had always picked up on his mood. "What do you mean?"

"You weren't very friendly. You hardly looked at her. Did she do something to piss you off?"

"No. I barely know her. How could she piss me off?"

"Something is wrong. I could feel the tension between y'all." Zach linked his hands across his stomach. "You've always had a thing for blondes and she's hot."

"Yeah. Right," Brent said, his voice flat.

Zach waved his hand in front of Brent's face. "Do you need an eye exam? She's stunning."

"You didn't see her arms."

"Her arms?" Zach's eyebrows drew together. "I'll be honest. I wasn't looking at her arms." A hint of a smile touched his lips. "I'm married, but I'm not dead."

Brent didn't smile at Zach's joke. "She has scars on the back of her arms."

Zach's smile quickly disappeared. "She was hurt?"

"Yeah. In a fire."

"My God," Zach whispered. "What a horrible thing to happen to her. She must have been terrified." He slowly straightened in his chair. "I can tell by the expression on your face that you didn't offer her any sympathy."

Brent hadn't given a thought to offering Robin any sympathy. Once her scars had been revealed, that's all he could see.

Zach shook his head. "So once again, you were an ass to a woman who didn't live up to your idea of perfection."

Brent rose and stormed over to the windows. He was really tired of his brother and sister telling him how he should feel.

He tensed when he heard Zach's footsteps behind him. "Brent—"

"I don't want to hear it. Michelle has already chewed me out today. I don't need the same thing from my brother."

Zach laid his hand on Brent's shoulder. Brent shrugged it off. "I know what I want. Why is that so wrong?"

"Because you're hurting yourself. You're looking for a perfect woman. She doesn't exist."

"Oh, you're a fine one to talk." Brent turned from the window and glared at Zach. "I saw your honeymoon pictures with Jade in her skimpy bikini. Your wife is gorgeous. And Michelle certainly didn't settle for ugly men. I'm not into guys, but I know how good-looking Andre and Nathan are."

"But Chelle and I didn't search out someone physically perfect. Yes, Jade is gorgeous. I'm very proud to have such a beautiful wife. But I fell in love with the woman inside, the one who's caring and loving and makes me laugh." Zach touched

Brent's shoulder again. "You can't base love on looks, Brent. Jade told me that while we were dating. It's true."

"I'm not talking about love. That doesn't even interest me. I don't want to be tied down to one woman."

"I didn't either, until I met Jade. She changed my life. When you meet the right woman, she'll change your life too."

"My life is fine as is."

Brent bristled at the look of pity in Zach's eyes. "I know what I'm doing."

"I hope so. I really do." Zach looked at his watch. "Jade's car is in the shop. I have to pick her up from work. What time do you want me here tomorrow night for the pictures?"

"I told the guys to be here at six."

Zach nodded. "I'm picking up Jade at noon tomorrow so she can get her car. I'll be here after that."

Brent waited, suspecting that his brother wanted to say more. Instead, Zach squeezed Brent's shoulder. "See you tomorrow."

Once Zach left, Brent turned back to the window. The sun would set soon. He had nothing planned tonight except to watch the football game. He could call any number of women and go out instead of going home. A delicious meal and a fast fuck would be good.

Except he didn't want to go out with any woman. He kept thinking of the way his stomach had dropped to his feet when he first saw Robin. He'd never had such a strong reaction so quickly to a woman. Her hair, her complexion, her eyes, her body…he thought he'd finally found the perfect woman.

Only she wasn't perfect. One look at her scars proved that.

He saw no reason to settle for almost perfection. He knew what he wanted when he took a woman to bed.

He wouldn't accept anything less.

Chapter Three

Michelle's illness couldn't have happened at a worse time. Brent was sorry she felt badly, yet he was also frustrated for now the website redesign fell on him. That meant a lot of time with Robin.

Brent splashed more wine into his glass. He'd set out refreshments on the desk, as per Michelle's instructions. Even while sick in bed, she'd jotted down duties for him and had Nathan deliver her list. She'd scrawled, *BE NICE TO ROBIN!* at the bottom of the paper. He'd frowned when he read that. Michelle was treating him as if he had no manners and didn't know how to be nice to a woman. He knew how to be *very* nice to a woman.

Of course, that kind of "nice" would never happen with Robin. Thinking of anything sexual with Robin made him shudder with revulsion.

Leaning back in his chair, he watched Nathan fiddle with his camera settings. Nathan had arrived half an hour ago with his cameras, tripod, and lights. Robin was due at any moment with the backdrops. Nathan said Andre would be here about seven, after he prepared soup for Michelle.

His sister had fallen into a strange relationship. Nathan and Andre had been lovers for four years before moving from Chicago to Fort Worth. Both men were bi, both of them had fallen for Michelle almost from the moment they saw her. She'd felt the same way about them. Instead of choosing between the two men, she'd asked both of them to live with her.

Brent sipped his wine. He'd had a couple of male lovers. It had been...interesting. While enjoyable, he much preferred the soft curves of a woman.

"Everything is set," Nathan said, dropping down in the chair next to Brent. "All I need now is a back drape and a model."

"Who's going to take *your* picture?"

"Andre. He knows my cameras. I won't let Michelle use them."

"You're wise. She's broken at least three cameras that I know of."

"She told me. That's why she doesn't touch mine."

Brent chuckled. "She'd seriously hurt us if she knew we're talking about her."

"Nah. Her bark is worse than her bite." Nathan grinned wickedly. "I love her bite."

"Too much information, Nathan. No sex talk about my sister."

Nathan poured a glass of Merlot for himself. "It hasn't been easy for you to accept mine and Andre's relationship with Michelle."

"To be honest, it wouldn't be easy for me to accept *anyone's* relationship with Chelle. I still see the freckle-faced brat when I look at her."

"I don't have a sister, but I'd probably feel the same way you do."

Brent rested his ankle on the opposite knee. "I'm surprised she agreed to you and Andre staying on as escorts."

"The money's too good to pass up. There's no sex. Ever. Michelle did put her foot down about that."

The bell over the front door rang. Brent recognized Warren's and Clarke's voices in the foyer. Ten of the escorts, counting Nathan and Andre, would be here tonight. The rest of them were either booked or had left town for the holiday weekend. Brent stood to greet the two men as the bell rang again. Peter and Rod followed Warren and Clarke into the room. Nathan could begin taking the pictures, if he had the back drapes Robin said she'd bring.

The bell rang yet again. Brent turned to see who else had arrived. Robin came through the doorway.

His stomach tightened into a big knot at the sight of her. She wore her hair down tonight. It flowed almost to her breasts in soft waves. The purple, long-sleeved sweater hugged her breasts, the slim jeans skimmed down her legs.

God, she was lovely.

Correction—she looked lovely standing there with the last rays of the setting sun shining on her through the window. Her clothes covered her flaws...flaws he couldn't forget.

Another man came in right behind Robin. Peter carried a large box, which he handed to Nathan.

"Your drapes," Robin said to Nathan after Brent introduced them. "I picked up sapphire, emerald, and ruby. I thought we could change out the drapes depending on which color would look best with the escort."

"Or maybe use a couple of different colors with each guy," Nathan said.

"Good idea. Will you take a few shots of each escort? I want Michelle to have a nice variety."

"No problem. I'm taking the pictures with both digital and film. I'll take five or six shots with each camera."

"Great." She looked at the men in the room. Her gaze paused a few seconds longer on Brent before she moved to the next escort. "Who wants to be first?"

Clarke raised his hand. "I'll be the guinea pig."

Brent returned to his chair and picked up his wineglass. Clarke was one of Coopers' Companions' newest escorts, a handsome twenty-nine-year-old with dark brown hair and eyes that were almost black. He'd moved to Fort Worth four months ago from Houston. Tall, well-built, great smile. It hadn't taken Zach long to hire Clarke after he'd applied for a job.

Clarke sat on the stool in front of the ruby drape. Robin adjusted the collar of his shirt, the lapels of his jacket. He seemed to like her personal attention, his smile friendly and flirtatious. A little bit *too* flirtatious, in Brent's opinion.

He gripped his wineglass tighter when Robin drew a comb from her back pocket and ran it through Clarke's hair. She stood close enough that he could lift his hands a few inches and cradle her breasts. The gleam in Clarke's eyes told Brent the escort wouldn't mind doing that at all.

She smiled and stepped back from Clarke. "Perfect."

"So I've been told," he said with a grin.

Every man in the room laughed, except Brent. All the muscles in his body bunched with the need to stride across the room and tear Robin away from Clarke.

He didn't understand why he felt so strongly about her touching another man. She meant nothing to him.

She moved to stand beside Nathan as he snapped the first picture of Clarke. "I'd like some pictures without his jacket too."

"How about without the shirt?" Robert called out, laughter evident in his voice.

Robin turned and shook her finger at the escort. "We're doing professional, not beefcake."

Daryl grinned. "Beefcake is more fun."

"Yeah," Rod agreed. "Bare chests will draw more attention."

His employees were certainly having fun teasing her. And it appeared she enjoyed it. Brent doubted Robin was ever in a room with *one* handsome, sexy man, much less seven at the same time. She was probably loving the attention.

Clarke slid off the stool and Peter took his place. Robin repeated her primping of the second man. She tugged on the hem of his dark brown pullover to straighten it.

"Wanna adjust my jeans too?" Peter asked.

Again, the men laughed. Brent still didn't find the teasing funny, even though Robin did. She laughed along with the escorts.

"You're too eager." She dragged the comb through Peter's hair. "I'll do shirts and hair. The rest is up to you."

"She is hot," Warren whispered behind Brent.

"Yeah," Rod said. "Maybe she'll want to go out for a drink after we're through."

"With both of us?"

"Why not?"

Brent gritted his teeth to keep from ordering his employees to keep their eyes — and everything else — off Robin.

Brent silently drank and watched every one of his escorts flirt shamelessly with Robin while Nathan snapped their pictures. He felt as if someone stood on either side of him, trying to jerk him in two. One person told him not to look at Robin or be attracted to her, that she wasn't perfect. The other person urged him to notice how her hair curled around her head, her sweater hugged her breasts, her jeans cupped her ass.

The wine wasn't helping the churning inside him. He seriously thought about hitting the hard liquor in the kitchen, when Robin turned to face him.

"Brent. You're the last one."

He didn't want to do this. He didn't want to sit on that stool and let Robin comb his hair and adjust his clothes. Since he was the last escort here, he didn't have a choice. He drained his wineglass and set it on the desk, then surged to his feet.

He sat on the stool and Robin stood before him. The conversation in the room faded into the background. Robin was the only person he heard, the only person he saw. Brent sat still as she slowly ran the comb through his hair. The scent of her cologne drifted to his nose…a musky smell that made him think of tangled sheets and entwined limbs. He lowered his gaze to her breasts. A hint of her nipples showed through her sweater.

He looked back at Robin's face in time to see her swallow. She touched his mustache with the tip of the comb's teeth. Her hand trembled.

Brent saw Andre approach from the corner of his eye. "Good evening, Brent."

The interruption dragged Brent's focus away from Robin. "Hey."

Andre smiled. "You must be Robin. I'm Andre." He gestured over his shoulder toward the desk. "I brought lasagna. Are you hungry?"

"Famished."

"Yeah, me too." Brent hopped down from the stool and strode toward the desk. He couldn't get away from Robin quickly enough.

* * * * *

The skin on the back of Robin's neck tingled. She tried to ignore the sensation, but knew Brent watched her. He didn't want her, yet it seemed to bother him that the other escorts were friendly to her.

Men could be so strange.

The last three escorts and Zach had arrived as she'd eaten Andre's delicious lasagna. She enjoyed the conversation and laughter of the men in the room. And the view. It certainly wasn't a hardship to watch ten very handsome men. They'd treated her like a sister one moment and flirted the next. She understood why Coopers' Companions was so successful. Zach, Brent and Michelle hired men who were not only good-looking, but fun, charming and conversed easily on many different subjects.

She'd be sorry when the photo session ended for she'd have no reason to see any of them again.

"Break time," Nathan said after he snapped the last picture of Reese. "The photographer has to take a leak." A sheepish look crossed his face when his gaze collided with Robin's. "Oops. Sorry."

Robin waved away his apology. "Just think of me as one of the guys."

"No way any of us can do *that*," Daryl said, playfully leering at her breasts.

She chuckled. "You have sisters, don't you?"

"Three."

"And you love to torment them."

"Every chance I get."

A pang of longing filled her heart. She'd always wanted a brother or sister. She didn't think she would've minded the tormenting as long as she had someone close to her who would always be there no matter what happened.

Robin noticed Zach collecting the used wineglasses on a tray. She followed behind him, stacking up dirty saucers and forks.

"You don't have to do that, Robin."

"I don't mind. I'll even wash them."

"No, you won't. We have a dishwasher."

She followed Zach to the large, airy kitchen. "I'll load the dishwasher if you'll bring the rest of the dishes."

"Brent and I will take care of the dishes. You have to help Nathan with the photos."

"Nathan deserves a break." She waved both hands at him in a "go away" motion. "Get the rest of the dishes."

Zach chuckled. "You're almost as bossy as my wife. Be right back."

Robin located a dish cloth first, then opened the dishwasher door. She straightened and took a step back, directly into a male body.

Robin didn't have to look to know Brent stood behind her. Her heart had begun to gallop as soon as she touched him. One strong arm encircled her waist, his fingers splayed across her stomach. His fly nestled between her buttocks. She could feel his cock hardening against her.

As quickly as he'd touched her, he released her. "Sorry," he muttered.

She turned in time to see him leave the kitchen. Robin sighed. How unfair that the one man who affected her so strongly was the one man who wanted nothing to do with her.

She knew it was a good thing that Brent was so turned off by her scars since she couldn't get involved with him anyway. She would never take the chance on another man getting hurt.

* * * * *

When Nathan snapped the last picture shortly after ten o'clock, Robin was ready to call it an evening. She was glad ten escorts showed up instead of the fifteen she and Michelle had discussed. Pictures of five more men would've taken at least another hour. Besides taking more time for the pictures, she didn't want to spend another hour with Brent staring at her.

She peeked at him as she made notes on her ever-present legal pad. He stood to the side, talking to his brother. All the men here tonight were gorgeous. Only one made her stomach feel as if it would drop to her feet any moment.

Gathering up her purse and laptop case, she walked over to the two brothers. Both faced her. Zach smiled. Brent didn't.

"I spoke with Nathan about finishing up the pictures after Thanksgiving," Robin said. "That works for him. Michelle will be well by then and I can get the pictures of the three of you."

"Did you get all the info you need from the guys tonight?" Zach asked.

Robin glanced at Brent before turning back to Zach. "No."

"Would you like my help?"

Robin smiled. "Thanks for the offer, but I have enough to get started. Michelle and I will work on the website next week. She can give me the rest of the escorts' information."

"If you change your mind, call here," Zach said. "Coopers' Companions is closed until Monday, but I'll check messages over the weekend."

Robin smiled. She really liked the eldest Cooper sibling. "Thanks, Zach. I appreciate that." She waved to the remaining escorts on her way to the front door, taking extra care not to look at Brent again. "Have a great holiday, guys."

Chapter Four

Brent scowled as he watched Robin head for the front door without a backward glance at him. She'd been all smiles for Zach and the guys still here, yet completely ignored him.

"Robin would like you a lot better if you'd lose the attitude."

Brent looked at his brother. His scowl deepened when he saw the amusement in Zach's eyes. "What the hell are you talking about?"

"You want her, but you don't want to want her."

"You're crazy, man."

"I saw your clinch in the kitchen. The look on your face said it all."

"And what kind of 'look' do you think I had?"

"Like you could've taken her right there on the counter, if y'all had been alone in the house."

"I want nothing to do with her."

"You can lie to yourself, but you can't lie to me. She's a great lady, Brent. Forget about Robin's so-called disfigurement and get to know her."

"You haven't seen her scars."

"It wouldn't matter to me if I had. I look at the *inside* of a person, Brent. You'd be a lot happier if you'd do the same."

Brent had heard this same sermon from Zach so many times, he'd lost count. "I'm outta here," he muttered. "See you Thursday." Brent walked away from his brother before Zach could say anything else.

Almost Perfection

* * * * *

The Dallas Mavericks were in the fourth quarter of their basketball game when Brent walked into the First and Ten Sports Bar. He stood in the doorway long enough to watch the Indiana Pacers steal the ball before making his way to the bar.

Brent slid onto the stool on the end. Trey tended bar tonight. The bartender had worked here for the last three or four months. Brent had tried to talk Trey into joining Coopers' Companions. With Trey's dark good looks and ease with people, he'd be a great escort. Trey always said no. Brent didn't know what Trey earned as a bartender, but doubted it equaled what he could make as an escort.

"Hey, Brent." Trey leaned on the bar in front of Brent. "Beer?"

"Yeah."

A cheer in the room drew Brent's attention to one of the large TVs. First and Ten had five wide-screen televisions scattered about the bar. Those, along with great food and generous drinks, made the sports bar a popular place. Women hung out here because men hung out here. Brent could always find a willing woman when he looked for one. There had been many times when he'd accepted a woman's invitation to her home.

Tonight, he wanted nothing to do with women...especially one.

Trey set a frosty mug of draft beer in front of Brent. "So, what's up? I don't usually see you in here on a Tuesday."

"I had to be at the office tonight."

"Problems?"

Brent sipped his beer. The cold brew slid smoothly down his throat. "We started taking pictures of the guys tonight for a new website. Michelle hired this woman to do the work. She's..." He stopped and took another drink while trying to decide how to describe Robin. "We don't get along."

"I got that." Trey leaned on the bar again. "Why not? Is she pushy? Conceited? Rude?"

Brent thought about Trey's questions. No, Robin wasn't any of those things. She was charming and friendly and lovely. Cuddling up to her ass in the kitchen for those few seconds tonight had given him an instant hard-on. Brent had always had an active sex drive. Becoming aroused had never been a problem. He didn't think he'd ever become so hard so quickly as when he had touched Robin.

"No, none of those. Robin is okay. We just don't click."

"Robin? Pretty name."

"She's a pretty woman." Brent moved his mug through the circle of condensation on the bar. "A *very* pretty woman. Blonde hair, hazel eyes, great body."

"She sounds perfect."

"She's far from perfect."

"What's wrong with her?"

Brent opened his mouth to tell Trey, but closed it again before saying anything. He had no right to talk badly about Robin to someone who didn't even know her. "It isn't important." Brent drained his mug and set it on the bar. "I'd better go."

"You don't want another?"

"Not tonight." He dug a ten-dollar bill from his pocket and tossed it on the bar. "Thanks for listening."

Trey smiled. "Any time."

Brent stepped out into the cool night. A cold front was due to blow in by two a.m., dropping the temperature at least forty degrees. It would barely get above freezing tomorrow. They'd get a hint of winter right in time for Thanksgiving.

The entire family would gather at Zach's and Jade's house for the big feast. Zach said Jade had planned the menu weeks ago and was looking forward to her first major holiday as a Cooper.

Brent slid behind the wheel of his car. He adored Jade. She made his brother happier than Zach had ever been in his life. That was reason enough for Brent to welcome Jade into the family.

He came to the intersection where he could either turn left to go to his condo, or right to go back to Coopers' Companions. Home held no appeal. He turned right.

Brent was still waiting for return emails from some of the escorts about the website pictures. He decided to check voice mail and email once more before he headed home.

He checked Coopers' Companions' email first. There were six inquiries for more information and one message for penis enhancement. Brent chuckled. He didn't need any help in *that* department. No woman had ever told him his cock was too small.

After forwarding the document Michelle had designed with the requested information to the six inquiries, Brent opened up his personal account. The rest of the escorts had answered his message about the pictures, all except for Jim and Rubin. That surprised him. Both men faithfully checked their messages on their fancy phones. Jim, especially, usually responded in less than ten minutes.

How strange that he hadn't.

Shrugging off his concern, Brent opened an email from one of the escorts. Jim had signed out until next week. If he'd decided to run away with a gorgeous woman for the long weekend, that was certainly his right. Brent was sure Jim would check in the first chance he could.

* * * * *

Robin dropped Reese's picture into place in her template. Nathan had promised he'd email her the digital pictures he'd taken tonight as soon as he got home. She'd been so wound up after the photo shoot and excited about Nathan's incredible photos, she'd decided to work on the Cooper website for a while. That "a while" had turned into hours.

The clock on her laptop showed her it was almost three a.m. Her eyelids were beginning to droop. If she didn't stop, she'd start making mistakes and have to do her work over again.

Robin saved her work and closed her computer's lid. A huge yawn made her jaw pop. Now that she'd decided to go to bed, she couldn't get there fast enough. Stripping off her clothes, she donned the large T-shirt she liked to sleep in, crawled between the sheets, and turned off the lamp. A gentle sigh escaped her lips as she closed her eyes.

An image formed behind her closed lids—the one of Brent sitting on the stool as she combed his hair. She saw those incredible blue eyes staring into hers, that luscious blond mane that fell almost to his shoulders. His hair was soft and thick. She'd imagined running her fingers through it, over and over, while she'd combed it.

The fantasies didn't stop there. She pictured tugging off the green T-shirt he'd worn tonight so she could touch his chest. He was lean, but with the strong shoulders and wide chest of a swimmer. She'd run her hands over his warm skin, maybe scratch him just a bit. A dash of pain with pleasure could be fun.

She wouldn't let him touch her yet, even though he'd try. First, she'd slowly remove the rest of his clothes, revealing his body a little at a time. She wanted to savor the first time she saw him completely nude. She had no doubt he would be magnificent.

By the time he was naked, his cock would be hard and ready for her. Robin saw herself dropping to her knees before him, taking his firm flesh in her mouth. She'd cradle his balls in her palm while her mouth slid up and down his shaft. She'd lick him thoroughly with her tongue, concentrating all around the head. Maybe she'd tease his anus with a wet fingertip. All those nerve endings in the sensitive area would come alive with some light stroking.

Robin rolled to her back and covered her eyes with her arm. She tugged up her T-shirt and slipped her other hand inside her panties to the warm, wet flesh between her thighs. She circled her clit with one finger as she imagined Brent pumping into her mouth. She'd bring him to the brink of orgasm before she pulled her mouth away from him.

Brent would object, but she'd kiss him, caress him, promise him more to come. He'd sit still and watch her take off her clothes. He'd palm her breasts, suck her nipples, as soon as she removed her bra. A whisk of his thumb, a swipe of his tongue, and she'd forget about the rest of her clothes while absorbing the pleasure of his mouth.

Robin moved her fingers over her labia, picked up her body's cream and spread it over her clit. She rubbed faster as she thought of Brent's mouth on her breast, her belly, her pussy. He'd make her come with his tongue before sliding his cock inside her channel. He'd fuck her with long, slow strokes...first in her pussy, then in her ass.

"Oh God!"

The orgasm shook her body from head to toes. Robin continued to caress her clit while her breathing slowed and her heart stopped racing. She opened her eyes and stared into the darkness. Her body still hummed from her climax. She knew how to touch herself, and where, to pleasure herself. Making love with Brent would be even better.

He might be a jerk, but she'd bet he knew how to touch a woman to make her forget every lover she'd ever had.

She hadn't been so attracted to a man in years. She'd dated, had even made love a few times, but she hadn't felt that kick-in-the-stomach desire since...

Stuart.

Robin squeezed her eyes closed again. She'd been so stupid to get involved with Stuart. She didn't want to think about him, yet she couldn't help it. Every time she looked in a mirror, she saw the result of her stupidity.

It was that result that would keep Brent away from her.

*****

Hey guys,

Michelle has decided to update the Coopers' Companions website. Y'all know my sister. When she makes up her mind about something, there's no stopping her. She wants the update NOW.

She's hired a graphic designer, Robin Howell, to do the work. Nathan will take the photos. He'll start the first set of pix tomorrow. Email or call my cell and let me know if you can make it. Otherwise, we'll do the rest after Thanksgiving.

Brent.

He read the email for the third time. So sweet little Robin was a graphic designer now. All she'd cared about in Colorado was skiing and having a good time. She'd not only moved away from her home state, she'd changed her whole life.

No problem. He'd followed her move from Colorado to Michigan to Texas. No matter where she decided to go, he'd find her.

After all, she belonged to him.

Some of his plans would have to be changed. He hadn't wanted to expose himself to Robin yet. He liked the idea of playing with her, of keeping her on edge until he was ready to take her.

He frowned. He didn't like her hanging around Coopers' Companions and all those men. Especially Brent Cooper. Brent was too attractive to women. He'd seen them fall all over the guy more than once. He couldn't allow her to get too close to Brent. A business relationship was okay. Anything other than that...

He liked Brent and would hate to hurt him. But he would do whatever he had to do to keep the woman he loved.

He'd killed once. He'd kill again in a heartbeat.

Chapter Five

The insistent ringing penetrated Robin's foggy brain. Reaching out one hand, she groped for the telephone receiver. She hit herself in the temple and muttered a soft curse before she found her ear. "'Lo?"

"Robin?" a feminine voice asked.

"Yeah." She pushed her hair out of her eyes. "Whoz this?"

"Jade Cooper. I assumed you'd be up by now. I'm sorry I woke you."

Robin glanced at the digital clock. 9:23. Normally, she would've been awake two hours ago. "That's okay." She sat up and stuffed a pillow behind her back. "I stayed up late working on Coopers' Companions' website."

"Zach told me you'd be working on it most of the weekend. That isn't acceptable. I want you to have dinner with us tomorrow."

Robin wasn't sure how to respond. She'd never expected an invitation to something reserved for family. "Dinner?"

"Michelle said you don't have any family here. A person shouldn't be alone on Thanksgiving."

Robin was used to being alone. She'd been alone most of her life. She'd mentioned in the few minutes she'd had with Michelle that she had no family. She hadn't expected Michelle to remember that, much less pass on the information to her sister-in-law. "I appreciate the invitation, Jade, but—"

"No buts, no excuses. You aren't going to work on Thanksgiving when I'm preparing enough food to feed half of Fort Worth. We're eating at one, but you can come over whenever you want to. Do you have a pen and paper to write down our address?"

It appeared Jade wouldn't take no for an answer. Spending the day with people would be nice, if it didn't include Brent. After her erotic fantasy last night, she didn't think she could face him without wanting to fulfill that fantasy. "I have a lot of work to do."

"You have to eat. You can take a break long enough for dinner. And I do mean a break. No work allowed. Michelle said you take your laptop everywhere. If I see it, I'll lock it in a closet."

Robin decided she'd revealed way too much personal information to Michelle. But she'd been so easy to talk to, so willing to listen. It had been a long time since Robin had clicked so quickly with another woman, even though they'd been together less than an hour.

"Are you ready for the address?" Jade asked.

Robin didn't know how to say no without hurting Jade. She wouldn't hurt Jade for anything. Reaching into the nightstand, she withdrew a pen and notepad. "I'm ready."

* * * * *

"Stop that!" Jade said, slapping at Brent's hand. "You'll mess up the arrangement."

Brent had hovered in the kitchen for the last ten minutes, picking at the food his sister-in-law was trying so hard to protect from his wandering fingers. "What arrangement? We're going to eat it anyway."

"We aren't going to eat until one." She slapped at him again when he reached for a piece of fudge. "No dessert until after the meal."

"You sound like my mother."

"I think your mother should've spanked you more often than she did." She grabbed both his hands so he could no longer reach any goodies. "Go watch the football game."

"It isn't on yet."

Jade rolled her eyes. Raising one fist, she waved it in front of his nose. "How would you like a black eye?"

She couldn't kill a bug with those gentle hands, but he went along with her. "I don't think I'd like that very much."

"Then get out of my kitchen."

"You want some help with him, Mom?" Breanna asked from behind Brent.

He turned to see Jade's daughter, hands on her hips. "You think you can take me, Talmage?"

"In a heartbeat, Cooper."

Brent doubted that. Breanna couldn't weigh much over one-twenty. He could see the amusement in her eyes. She enjoyed their playful arguing as much as he did.

Holding back his laughter was getting harder. Brent held up his hands in surrender. "Okay, I give. I can't fight both of you. I'll leave peacefully."

The doorbell rang as Brent left the kitchen. A family member would simply walk in, not ring the doorbell. He couldn't imagine who would be here on a holiday. "I'll get it, Jade."

He opened the door, and almost swallowed his tongue when he saw Robin on the other side.

It took him a moment to remember how to speak. "Hey."

"Hi," she said, her voice soft and hesitant.

The wind teased her hair about her shoulders. She wore a brown trench coat that fell past her knees. Brown boots peeked out from the hem of her dark jeans.

His gaze traveled back up her body to her face. Her cheeks were pink. Whether from makeup or the cold weather, he didn't know.

Cold weather. *Shit!* Brent quickly stepped aside so Robin could enter the house. "Come in."

"Thanks."

Brent closed the door behind her. He watched as she looked around the open concept space. The living room was to their right, the kitchen and dining room to their left.

"What a beautiful home."

"Zach's a great carpenter."

She turned to face him. "Zach built this?"

Brent nodded. "With some help from Michelle and me. I did the grunt work. She did most of the painting."

"Is Michelle here?"

"She's picking up our mom. They should be here soon."

"Hi, Robin," Jade called out. "I'm so glad you could make it."

"Thanks for inviting me."

"You aren't here to work on the website with Michelle?" Brent asked.

Robin shook her head. "Jade invited me to dinner."

Jade walked toward them, wiping her hands on a dish towel. "And I told her no working today. Did you bring your laptop?"

Robin laughed. "No."

"Good. I fixed a spot in the closet to hide it, just in case."

She would have dinner with them, which meant he'd be around her most of the day...smelling her perfume, looking into those incredible hazel eyes, thinking about how her breasts would feel in his hands.

Shit!

He didn't want to want her, but didn't know how to change his feelings. He'd never fantasized so much about a woman in his life. He'd laid awake in his bed last night, long after he'd turned off the lights, and imagined her lying beside him, bare skin to bare skin...

"Brent," Jade said, breaking into his thoughts. "Take Robin's coat please."

His ears turned warm at Jade's reminder. He shouldn't have needed it. A gentleman always offered to take a lady's coat. "Sorry," he muttered.

He helped Robin out of her coat and hung it in the closet by the front door as the women went into the kitchen. Simply being around Robin was messing with his head.

Another good reason to stay away from her.

The front door opened behind him. Zach entered, carrying a sack from the local supermarket. This was his brother's second trip to the store this morning for "just one more thing", as Jade had put it. He set the bag on the island that divided the kitchen and living room.

"This had better be the last thing you need. The store closes at noon."

"It is." Jade wrapped one arm around Zach's neck and kissed him soundly. "Thank you."

"I want more than a kiss for running all these errands."

"Later. I promise."

She kissed him again. Zach cradled Jade's cheek in his hand. He rubbed his thumb across her skin, tenderly caressing her as they kissed. A strange tightness filled Brent's chest. He wondered what it would be like to commit to one woman, to devote himself totally to her for the rest of his life.

His gaze wandered to Robin. She stood next to Breanna, both of them watching the couple's loving display. A look of longing filled her eyes. She obviously wanted the same kind of relationship with a man.

Not Brent. He didn't want to get involved with Robin or any other woman. He was happy with the life he had now and planned to leave everything the same.

*****

Michelle had arrived with her mother shortly after Brent turned on the television. Robin thought Colleen Cooper was a stunning woman. Tall, blonde hair, impeccably dressed and just as friendly as she was lovely. Her eyes were amber, so the siblings must have inherited their blue eyes from their father.

When the talk turned more bawdy with comparisons of men and their "assets", Colleen freely gave her opinion too. She admitted she'd had quite a few dates since her husband died. Several of those dates had included sex. Michelle's expression clearly said she couldn't believe her mother was talking so openly about lovers.

"You think I died when your father did?" Colleen asked.

"No, of course not. I just never... I mean, you didn't... I don't..." Michelle sputtered to a stop.

"You never think of your parents having sex," Breanna said.

"Exactly!" Michelle appeared relieved for the help. "Thanks, Bre."

Jade and Colleen exchanged a look before they both laughed.

Robin stood to the side, quietly chopping celery for the vegetable tray and listening to the conversation. She'd never been part of a large holiday meal. Uncomfortable at first to intrude on a family get-together, she quickly got over her uneasiness. The women had made her feel very welcome, as if they all truly wanted her here.

The front door opened again. Robin automatically glanced up when she heard male voices. She recognized Nathan and Andre. Michelle had mentioned that the two men had gone to the airport to pick up Andre's brother, Sandro, who had flown in from Italy for a visit. The dark-haired hunk must be Sandro.

She'd learned by bits and pieces of conversation that Michelle lived with Andre and Nathan. She could see why. A woman would have a difficult time choosing between the two if she based her choice on looks alone. Both men were tall, well built and very handsome.

Robin had been around more good-looking men this week than she had in her life.

Michelle gave Nathan and Andre quick hugs, then smiled at Sandro. His white teeth flashed as he returned her smile. Taking her hand, he lifted it to his lips and kissed the back.

"*Piacere*," he said. "*Come mi ha detto mio fratello, sei affascinante.*"

Robin heard Michelle's soft gasp. She could understand why Michelle would lose her breath. What woman wouldn't love a handsome man speaking to her in Italian?

Michelle's smile widened. "I don't know what you said, but yes."

Sandro chuckled. "I said I am pleased to meet you, and you are as charming as my brother said."

"You shouldn't say yes so quickly, *bella*," Andre said. He slid his arm around Michelle's waist. "Sandro is my rogue brother. He loves the ladies."

"What is there not to love? I am surrounded by beauty."

Sandro's dark gaze touched each woman in turn when Andre said their names. He passed Robin to look at Breanna, but quickly returned to her. His tongue touched his bottom lip as he nodded at her. Robin's tummy fluttered at the obvious interest in his eyes.

Brent stepped into the kitchen in time to see what Sandro had done. His eyes narrowed, his lips tightened. If Robin didn't know better, she'd think Brent was jealous of Sandro's attention to her.

"My brother, Sandro," Andre said to the two men after Zach also stepped into the kitchen. "Michelle's brothers, Zach and Brent."

Sandro stepped forward, hand outstretched. "A pleasure."

Smiling, Zach shook Sandro's hand. "Welcome. Is this your first trip to America?"

"No. I visited Andre when he lived in Chicago, but it has been many years. This trip gives me the chance to use my English, eh?"

"Your English is very good," Jade said.

Sandro smiled. "Thank you." He reached for her hand. "Jade, yes?"

She nodded.

"You are as lovely as the jewel."

He started to kiss her hand but Zach gently pulled it away from Sandro. "Sorry. I'm the only one who gets to kiss her hand."

"You are lucky."

Zach tugged Jade in front of him and wrapped his arms around her waist. "Yes, I am."

Sandro turned to Brent and offered his hand. "Brent. A pleasure."

Brent shook his hand, but Robin noticed the scowl remained on his face.

"I don't know about anyone else," Breanna said, "but I'm hungry. How soon do we eat, Mom?"

"Now. Everyone grab something and set it on the bar."

The bar between the kitchen and dining room was soon filled with platters and bowls of food. Jade announced the meal would be buffet style. That would give everyone more room at the table, and no one would have to pass bowls back and forth instead of enjoying their meal.

China, linen napkins and fresh flowers graced the table. Jade had even made placecards. Robin found her place and noticed she was seated between Brent and Sandro. She wondered if Jade had done that on purpose so she sat between the two unattached males.

Once everyone had filled their plates and were seated, Zach raised his wineglass. "Bear with me while I get mushy." He waited until the chuckles had died before speaking again. "I thank my beautiful wife for the incredible meal—"

"Which we can't eat since you're talking," Brent said with laughter in his voice.

Michelle shot him a dirty look from across the table. Brent gave her an innocent grin. The grin remained on his lips when he looked at Robin. She returned it. She liked the teasing Brent much better than the surly one.

"And thanks to all of you for being here." Zach lifted his wineglass higher. "To family and friends."

The cool wine slid down Robin's throat and warmed her tummy, but not as much as the hot look in Brent's eyes. His gaze shifted from her throat to her eyes and back while she swallowed.

He picked up his fork to eat, breaking the spell. Robin released a shaky breath and picked up her own fork. Her fantasy from last night popped back into her head. She wished it could come true, but knew it never would. As soon as Brent remembered about her scars, he'd lose any desire for her.

* * * * *

It was a nice house…small but neat. Robin had always kept a neat house. He knew she was renting and not buying. A computer genius could find out all kinds of things online. His skills on the computer had sharpened in the last seven years. He had no doubt he could hack into any system that he chose.

He loved the feeling of power that gave him.

Strolling through the living room, he touched her furnishings as he passed them. He picked up a pillow from the couch, closed his eyes and took a deep sniff. A trace of her perfume lingered.

He wandered from room to room. Dishes sat in a drainer on the kitchen cabinet. A basket in the laundry room contained folded towels. Papers were scattered across her dining room table. He sorted through them carefully, not wanting to disturb their order. She'd jotted down notes for her graphic design jobs. The notes for Coopers' Companions' website lay on top.

Robin was very talented. He'd looked at all the websites she'd created. She had a great eye for color, for design. She'd do an incredible job when she decorated their home.

Soon.

He wasn't ready to come for her yet. First he wanted to play. She deserved to suffer a little for sending him to prison. She never should have done that. He loved her. He'd do anything for her. Surely she knew that.

He'd planned for weeks exactly what to do. His plan was brilliant.

Habits were hard to break. Robin always hid anything valuable beneath a pile of sweaters on the top shelf of her closet. Her habits hadn't changed. He found her laptop beneath a blue turtleneck.

A few minutes later he turned off the computer and replaced it in the exact spot he'd found it. One more item and he'd be through.

He left Robin's house the same way he'd entered. Whistling a tune from her favorite movie, he walked down the street toward his vehicle.

Chapter Six

Brent remembered a story Zach told him about his first date with Jade. He'd escorted her to her hospital's one hundredth anniversary gala. She'd worn an emerald dress that hugged her curves and drew the eyes of every man in the room. The head of surgery had danced so close to Jade, Zach had been tempted to shove the doctor's nose up his ass.

Brent felt the same way now about Sandro.

The man had hung close to Robin through the entire meal. After everyone had stuffed themselves past being able to walk, Zach announced since the women cooked, the men got to clean. Sandro didn't have to help since he was a guest. Instead, he plopped down on one of the couches between Robin and Breanna. He was polite to Jade's daughter but most of his attention centered on Robin. Brent could hear her laugh several times while he and Zach cleaned off the dining room table. Each giggle made him want to wrap his hands around Sandro's neck.

"I have a solution," Zach said.

Brent stopped stacking plates and looked at his brother. "A solution for what?"

"Your jealousy."

Brent glared at Zach. "I don't know what you're talking about."

"Your eyes turned green an hour ago. It's eating you up that Robin is talking to Sandro. You need to get her away from him. Ask her out."

Deciding not to comment on Zach's suggestion, Brent picked up the stack of plates and carried them to Nathan, who loaded the dishwasher while Andre put away the food. Brent went back to the dining room for another load of dishes to avoid his brother. That didn't work. Zach followed.

"I wouldn't waste any time if I were you."

"I have no desire to go out with Robin."

"C'mon, bro, you can't lie to me. I see the way you look at her. I don't blame you for being attracted to her. If I wasn't married, *I'd* ask her out."

Brent was a second away from ordering Zach to stay away from Robin, but caught himself before he said anything. That would make it sound as if Brent wanted to be with her. Which he didn't. That didn't mean some Italian Casanova had the right to sniff around her as if she were a bitch in heat.

"Drop it, Zach."

Zach frowned. Brent tensed, ready to argue if he had to. Zach remained silent as he cleared more items off the table and took them to the kitchen.

With everything put away and the kitchen spotless, the men joined the women and Sandro in the living room. Nathan and Andre flanked Michelle on the second couch. Zach dropped to the floor in front of the recliner where Jade sat. His mother sat in the other recliner. Brent would have to bring a chair from the dining room or sit on the floor too.

He chose the floor, right next to Robin's feet.

"Y'all timed that perfectly," Jade said. "The Cowboys game is about to start."

Zach wrapped one hand around Jade's calf. "My timing is always perfect." He nipped her knee through her jeans.

"Oh, jeez." Breanna rolled her eyes. "There they go again. Go to your room if you're gonna get sickening."

"It isn't sickening to love my wife."

"It is when you love her in front of all of us."

Brent paid no attention to his brother or Breanna. He'd rather look at Robin than listen to their playful bickering.

From the corner of his eye, he could see her glance at him every few minutes when Sandro wasn't talking to her. Each time she did, Brent returned her look. He wished he knew what she was thinking, if she enjoyed Sandro's attention as much as she appeared to.

The constant seesawing confused him. He'd never been uncertain about a woman. If he wanted her, he had her. If he didn't want her, he didn't give her another thought. It should be the same way with Robin. He didn't understand why it wasn't.

Robin stood at the end of the first quarter and tapped Jade on the shoulder. The two women went into the kitchen. The sound of the television kept Brent from hearing what they said. They spoke for several moments, then Jade hugged Robin. He watched Robin follow Jade to the coat closet.

Robin smiled at everyone. "Thanks so much for having me here today."

Zach stood, took Robin's coat from her and held it while she slipped it on. "It was our pleasure. You're always welcome here."

"I appreciate that." She looked straight at Brent. "Goodbye."

He acknowledged her goodbye with a nod. Robin stepped outside. She paused on the porch to button her coat. The cold wind whipped around her and she shivered. It would take her some time to adjust to the forty-degree temperature drop. She'd grown up in the Colorado cold and spent seven years in Michigan, but her system had grown used to the warm temperatures in the short time she'd lived in Texas.

She dug her keys out of her coat pocket and hurried down the steps to her car. Her hand trembled from the cold. It took her two tries before she could put the key in the ignition. She turned the key and received nothing but a grinding sound.

"Oh, no, don't do this to me. Not today."

She turned the key again and received the same grinding sound. She knew nothing about cars, but thought she wouldn't get any sound at all if she had a dead battery. That had to mean something more serious was wrong.

"Damn, damn, damn."

Robin had no choice but to call her insurance's roadside service for help. She removed her cell phone from the glove compartment and lifted the lid. No bars.

"Great. This gets better and better."

Releasing a heavy sigh, Robin opened the door. It would've blown shut on her leg if she hadn't caught it in time. A bruised leg on top of a dead car would *really* make her day.

She hurried back up the porch steps and rang the doorbell. She blew on her hands and stomped her feet to try to get some warmth circulating in her body. Skiing in Colorado had never left her this cold because she'd dressed appropriately for the weather. A lightweight trench coat wasn't enough for thirty-five degrees.

Zach opened the door. "Robin. You okay?"

"My car won't start and I can't get a signal on my cell. May I use your phone?"

"Come in."

Blessed warmth greeted her inside the house. She silently thanked whoever invented central heating.

"What's wrong?" Zach asked.

"It won't start. All I get is a grinding sound. That's not the battery, is it?"

"Brent and I will take a look. You stay in here where it's warm."

"You don't have to tell me that twice."

Zach gave her arm a quick squeeze as he passed her. "Have some coffee. We won't be long."

Robin accepted the mug of coffee from Jade. She wrapped both hands around the warm ceramic as she watched the two men through a window. She heard an even slower grinding when Zach tried to start her car. That didn't sound good at all.

Brent pulled his SUV over and opened the hood. He connected jumper cables to the battery and Zach tried starting Robin's car again. It didn't work.

Damn, damn, damn.

A few minutes under the hood and both men came back in the house. Neither looked happy.

"I think it's your fuel pump," Brent said. "Mom's car acted the same way when her fuel pump went out last year."

Fuel pump. Great. That probably isn't something my roadside service will fix.

Zach took off his jacket and draped it over the back of the recliner where his mother sat. "I doubt if you can find anyone to check it on Thanksgiving."

"I doubt I can either."

"I have a great mechanic. I'll call him in the morning and see if he can do a rush job."

"I appreciate that, Zach. May I use your phone to call a cab?"

"You aren't calling a cab," Brent said. "I'll take you home."

Robin hated having to depend on someone for help. She'd made it on her own for years, ever since she left Colorado seven years ago. Besides, she didn't think riding in Brent's vehicle with his scent surrounding her would be a good idea. He hadn't exactly sent her warm, loving looks today. "I live in the Hulen area. That's a long way from here. I don't want to be any trouble."

"You aren't any trouble. Besides, I doubt if you could get a cab to drive out here to the boonies anyway. Zach built his house as far out as he could and still be in the Metroplex."

A grin tugged at her lips. Brent could be funny when he chose to be. She liked that side of him. "Thank you. I appreciate it."

"Here," Jade said behind her. Robin turned to see Jade holding out a foil-wrapped plate. "A snack for later. I put some fudge in there too since you seemed to like it so much."

"I love it, but my waistline doesn't."

Jade waved her hand as if erasing Robin's comment. "You have to gain weight over the holidays. It's a law."

Robin thought Jade the nicest woman she'd ever met. All the ladies of the Cooper family had been so kind to her. "Well, I wouldn't want to break any laws. Thank you."

Brent held the front door open for her. Robin stepped out into the biting wind. First thing on her agenda next week would be to buy a heavier coat.

"Do you need anything out of your car?" Brent asked.

Robin shook her head. "My wallet, keys and cell phone are in my pockets. I'm good."

She accepted his hand to help her into his SUV. He jogged around the front of the vehicle and climbed into the passenger seat. One flick of his wrist and the SUV started.

"I know you're cold. It'll take a minute or so for the heater to get warm."

"I'm fine."

Brent backed out of his parking spot and turned the SUV down the long lane to the highway. "I see you shivering. This cold snap caught you by surprise, huh?"

"Going from seventy-five degrees one day to thirty-five the next definitely caught me by surprise."

Brent chuckled. "Welcome to North Texas."

"I didn't think it got this cold here."

"Temperatures in November can range from the twenties to the eighties."

"I'd prefer the eighties."

"You're gonna have to toughen up to live in Texas."

Robin could see his lips twitch, as if he were trying to keep from laughing. He seemed to be a lot happier when he teased her. "I'm tough enough, thank you."

"Where did you live before you moved to Texas?"

"How do you know I'm not a native?"

He gave her a look that clearly said, "Give me a break." Turning his gaze back to the road, he made a left onto the main highway. "You don't have a Texas accent."

"Oh." She couldn't deny that fact. "I grew up in Colorado. I spent seven years in Michigan before I moved here."

"Both places that have brutal winters. Don't you have a heavier coat?"

"I didn't think I'd need it here. I gave away most of my winter clothes before I left Michigan." She moved her feet closer to the heater vent. "Believe me, I'm going shopping first thing Monday."

"You aren't going to fight the crowds on Black Friday?"

"There is no such thing as a sale good enough to make me stand in line for two hours to pay."

"Michelle usually goes. I guess she won't this year since Sandro is here. She'll feel like she has to play hostess."

Robin hadn't considered that Michelle wouldn't be able to help her tomorrow. She'd hoped to get the information on the rest of the escorts so she could input it for the website. She'd picked out her favorite pictures from the ones Nathan had taken, but wouldn't upload them without Michelle's approval.

She had updates to do for other clients. She could work on those while waiting to get back together with Michelle.

Robin gave Brent her address when they drew closer to the Hulen Street exit off Interstate 20. He obviously knew the area well for he didn't ask for directions to her street. She watched his hands on the wheel. Tan, long fingers, a dusting of blond hair on the back. His hands weren't soft. They bore the calluses of a man who did physical work. He wouldn't get those rough hands from sitting behind a desk at Coopers' Companions.

She imagined those calloused hands coasting over her breasts, urging her nipples to harden...

"If you aren't going shopping," Brent said, "what will you do the rest of the weekend?"

His question threw a bucket of cold water on her erotic fantasy. "Work. I have updates to do for a few clients. And I want to work more on your website."

"You still need the guys' information to do that, don't you?"

"Yes, but there are some other things I can do first."

He slowed as a car exited the street in front of him. "Your street is next, right?"

"Yes. Turn left. Fourth house on the right."

He made the turn and drove slowly down the residential street. Robin loved this area. The houses were older, but well maintained with beautiful lawns. She chose to rent first to give herself time to find the perfect house to buy. She'd looked at several. So far, none of them had been "the one".

Brent pulled into her driveway and shut off the motor. "Do you want my help with the guys' information?"

She would appreciate having it, but didn't want to put Brent out on a holiday. "That's okay. I'm sure you'd rather be with your family today."

"I was with them earlier. If you need my help, I'm available."

She'd love to get more done on the website, as long as Brent didn't mind helping her. "Are you sure?"

"Will you make me a cup of coffee?"

Robin smiled. "That I can do."

"Then let's get to work."

Chapter Seven

Brent expected Robin to have a neat, clean house. That's exactly what he saw when he followed her through the front door.

His mother had insisted all three of her children learn to cook, clean and do laundry. Brent excelled at all those duties, even though he got out of them as often as possible. He'd be the first to admit he liked a neat home, but didn't want to clean it. He'd rather pay a cleaning service to come in twice a week to vacuum and dust and all those other tasks he hated.

"I have my paperwork spread over the dining room table," Robin said, untying the belt to her coat. Brent stepped behind her and took it as she slipped it from her shoulders. She smiled at him. "Thanks."

"Where do you want this?"

"On the coat tree by the door."

Brent hung up her coat, then removed his jacket. When he turned back to Robin, he caught her watching him. She quickly looked away.

Awareness surged between them. Brent felt it and had no doubt Robin felt it too. It almost crackled in the air.

"I'll start the coffee."

Robin walked out of the room, leaving Brent standing by the coat tree. He could wait for her to come back or follow her. He chose the latter.

He stood in the doorway of the small kitchen and watched her take a container of coffee from the refrigerator. She measured an amount for the coffeemaker and added water. After she took mugs out of the cabinet, she turned. Her eyes widened slightly. "I didn't know you were there."

Brent hooked his thumbs in the front pockets of his jeans and leaned against the doorway. "Did I scare you?"

"No. I just...didn't know you were there."

Her cheeks turned a becoming shade of pink. How refreshing to see a woman blush. The women Brent normally dated didn't know how to blush.

"The coffee will be ready in a couple minutes. Do you want to get started?"

Now there's a loaded question. He could imagine all kinds of ways to "get started", none of which he would mention. "Sure."

He followed her to the dining room. Piles of papers, pens and notepads covered the surface. This was obviously her work area, though he didn't see her laptop. "Where's your computer?"

"I hide it in my closet when I leave the house. I've never had any trouble in this neighborhood and neither have my neighbors." She shrugged. "A leftover habit from a long time ago."

"Better to be safe than sorry, as the cliché goes."

"Yes. That's true." She cleared her throat. "Sit down and I'll get the coffee. Do you take anything in yours?"

"Black is fine."

Robin hurried back to the kitchen. Every time her eyes met Brent's, it felt as though hundreds of butterflies took flight in her stomach. She hated that feeling. Despite the heat she sometimes saw in his eyes, nothing could ever develop between Brent and her.

She poured their coffee and carried the two mugs into the dining room. Brent sat at the table, reading from the printout she'd made of Coopers' Companions' opening page.

"This looks great." He smiled as he accepted the mug from her. He took a cautious sip of the hot brew. "Talented and you can make great coffee too. I'm impressed."

Robin laughed. "I'm full of surprises."

"I'm sure you are."

"Did you see the other pages?" she asked, ignoring his comment, which could be taken two ways.

"Not yet. I like the way you have Zach, Michelle and me on the opening page." He pointed to a square box on the sheet. "I assume this will be our picture."

Robin nodded. "People like photos. They want to know who they're dealing with. That's why I wanted pictures of the three Coopers as well as the escorts." She sorted through some papers and pulled out a sheet. "Since there are thirty escorts, I'm setting them up ten to a page. A lot of people still have dial-up Internet service. Too many photos on one page and it'll load too slowly."

"Which means someone could get disgusted at waiting and close the page."

"Exactly. We don't want that to happen." She pointed to Clarke's name on the sheet. "The escort's name will be beneath the picture. When someone clicks on the picture, she'll be taken to his individual page. She'll see a different, larger picture, plus his information—height, weight, interests, favorite color, name of dog, whatever you want listed."

"Have you completed a page yet?"

"I've done Clarke's since I had his pictures. I picked my favorites of the ones Nathan sent me, but won't post them until I get Michelle's approval."

"You'll have to settle for my approval. I doubt if Michelle will have any time to help you for at least a week with Andre's brother visiting."

"Your approval is fine. And anything we decide on can be changed later."

She located Clarke's page in her papers and turned it so Brent could see. "How's this?"

She silently sipped her coffee as Brent picked up Clarke's sheet and studied it. Her ego would love it if he approved it as is, but she had no problem with making changes. A client's vision and hers often differed. If the client wanted something totally outrageous that had nothing to do with the product or service, she would try to gently steer her or him in the direction that would be the best for business. Otherwise, she followed the client's wishes exactly.

"I like it. A lot."

His approval pleased her. "Thanks."

"I like the layout, the pictures you picked out, everything. I can't imagine Michelle would disagree with me."

"Then shall I follow that format with all the escorts' pages?"

"Yeah. Looks good."

"Okay." She pulled a legal pad in front of her and picked up a pen. "I'll need the names of the rest of your escorts. Do you know their ages?"

Brent nodded. "Sheldon Baker is twenty-nine, Pierce —"

He stopped when Robin's cell phone rang. "Excuse me."

"Sure."

Robin stood and removed her phone from her pants pocket as she strolled toward the living room. She didn't recognize the number, but it could be a client calling from a different number than one she was used to seeing. "Hello?"

"Robin?"

"Yes."

"It is Sandro."

She stopped walking. "Sandro?"

"*Si.* I am calling to make sure you arrived at your home safely. You are all right?"

"Yes, I'm fine."

"That is good. When Brent did not return, I asked Michelle for your phone number. I hope you do not mind."

"No, of course not. It's very sweet of you to be concerned."

"I do not wish anything bad to happen to you, *bella*. I would like to get to know you better while I am here. Will you dine with me tomorrow evening?"

Robin didn't know how to answer his question. She hadn't expected him to ask her out so quickly.

"You are not involved with anyone, no?"

"No, I'm not involved with anyone."

"Then dine with me."

"Sandro, I'm flattered. Truly. But I barely know you."

"It is a good way to get to know me, *si*?"

Robin chuckled. He was definitely persistent. And charming. And very handsome. "May I call you back? Brent and I are working right now."

"Oh. I did not realize you had work to do with Brent. I am sorry to disturb you."

"That's fine. But I do need to get back to work."

"Then I shall wait for you to call me back. *Ciao, bella.*"

Robin closed her phone. A soft smile curved her lips. In her solitary job, she didn't get the chance to meet many single men. How nice to have one ask her to dinner. She hadn't been out to dinner with a handsome man in weeks.

She turned to go back to the dining room. Brent stood directly behind her. She abruptly stopped or she would've run into him.

"What did Sandro want?" he asked.

"You eavesdropped on my conversation?"

"I didn't eavesdrop. I could hear you. You're only a few feet from the dining room table."

"Oh." She slipped her phone back in her pants pocket. "He said he was concerned we didn't make it here since you didn't return to Zach's house."

"That's all he wanted?"

She didn't like the tone of his voice. He almost sounded like a jealous lover. "It's none of your business what he wanted."

Brent scowled. He turned his head and blew out a breath. The scowl was gone when he looked at her again, yet his eyes clearly showed displeasure. "Did he ask you out?"

"I don't see where that's any of your business."

"No, it probably isn't." He took a step closer to her. "I'd still like to know if he asked you out."

His gaze passed over her face, her lips. Her heart began doing a jig in her chest. "Why?" she asked, barely above a whisper.

He tilted up her chin with one fingertip. "This is why."

His lips were warm and soft when they touched hers. Robin's eyes drifted closed. Brent didn't move his lips. He simply pressed them against hers, so sweetly that the kiss made her heart ache.

He lifted his head. The warmth of his kiss still touched her lips. He stared into her eyes as he ran his thumb over her bottom lip.

"God, a man could drown in your eyes."

She felt the same way about his. They were the most amazing blue she'd ever seen.

His thumb dipped between her lips. "One taste of you isn't enough."

"For me either."

Cradling her jaw with both hands, he tipped up her chin another inch. "Then there's no reason I shouldn't kiss you again."

Robin couldn't think of a single reason why he shouldn't. She sighed softly and parted her lips. The tip of Brent's tongue touched each corner of her mouth...teasing, playing.

Tempting.

His breath coasted over her lips before he covered them with his own. The first kiss had been a gentle introduction. This one was an invitation for more...an invitation Robin was only too happy to accept. She clutched Brent's waist as he deepened the kiss. His lips glided over hers, his tongue eased between them. His mouth moved one way, then the other, dropping soft, drugging kisses on her lips.

Robin slid her hands up his chest, over his shoulders, around his neck. She tilted her head, parted her lips farther at the urging of his tongue. It darted into her mouth and mated with hers.

She felt the tightening of his hands on her face. Then, slowly, he lowered his hands to drift across her collarbone and down to her breasts. Each mound received a gentle squeeze.

Robin threw back her head when Brent nuzzled the sensitive area beneath her ear. One arm encircled her waist and tugged her closer to him. The ridge of his hard cock pressed against her mound.

Before she could say how much she wanted him, his mouth covered hers again. No longer sweet and soft, this kiss devoured her mouth. He swept his tongue across her teeth, tickled her own tongue. He thrust his tongue into her mouth, again and again. Robin nipped it with each thrust.

"Jesus, you're hot," he muttered. Grasping one buttock, he pulled her even tighter against his shaft. He shifted from side to side, brushing her mound with his hard flesh. "I want to be inside you."

"Yesssss."

He spun her around and pulled her back against his front. Robin reached up and wrapped her arms around his neck again, leaving her body completely open for his touch. He nibbled up and down her neck as he caressed her breasts. Each pass of his thumbs across her nipples caused her breath to hitch. Moisture pooled between her thighs. Her pussy clenched when he tugged her nipples between his thumbs and forefingers.

"Do you like this?" he whispered in her ear.

Goose bumps scattered across her skin at the feel of his warm breath. "Yes."

"Do you want more?"

She wanted to yell, "Hell, yes!" Instead, she pushed her ass against his cock.

"My God, I've got to get inside you."

He grabbed the hem of her sweater and yanked it over her head. Robin waited for him to unfasten her bra next. Nothing happened.

A cold chill skittered down her spine. She knew he was looking at the scars on her back.

Robin whirled around to face him. He quickly lifted his gaze to her face, but not before she had time to verify her suspicions.

She wasn't sure how to describe the emotion in his eyes. It looked like a cross between disgust and pity. She wanted neither.

She swept up her sweater off the floor and pulled it back over her head. "Get out," she said flatly.

"Robin—"

"Get out *now*."

He ran one hand through his hair. "Will you let me explain what—"

"There is no explanation. You saw my scars and they disgusted you, exactly the way I knew they would." She crossed to the front door and opened it wide, ignoring the cold that swirled around her feet. "Get out."

He glanced toward the dining room. "What about the website?"

"I'll work with what I have and contact Michelle Monday."

His obvious stalling angered her even more. "I'm not paying to heat the outside, Brent. *Get out.*"

Slowly, he walked toward the door. He took his jacket from the coat tree and shrugged into it, looking at her face the entire time. She saw regret in his eyes now.

It was way too late for regrets.

He reached toward her cheek. She jerked her head back so he couldn't touch her. His hand fell to his side. "I wish you'd let me stay," he said softly.

"That isn't an option."

Brent stepped through the open door. Robin couldn't resist telling him exactly what she thought of him before he left. "You know what, Brent? I feel sorry for you. You're physically perfect and expect everyone around you to be the same. It doesn't work that way. There are so many wonderful people in the world who will never pass your idea of perfection. It's a shame you'll never get to know them. Your life would be so much richer if you'd open your eyes and your mind."

She slammed the door before he could say anything. Closing her eyes, she leaned her forehead against the cool wood. It felt as if a giant fist squeezed her heart. The pain was her own fault. She never should have let her developing feelings for Brent blossom, knowing he couldn't return them. Sex was easy. His hard cock pressed against her proved that. Tenderness, compassion, understanding…those were more difficult. And impossible for him.

Work would help her. She always felt better when she stayed busy. She pushed herself away from the door and headed for her bedroom to get her laptop. She'd do as much on Coopers' Companions' site as she could before she contacted Michelle for help.

Light from her two bedside lamps filled the room when she flipped up the wall switch. She took two steps into the bedroom, and froze. Her heart jumped in her chest. A roaring filled her ears. Chills raced through her body, leaving her trembling and unable to move.

A small box sat in the middle of her bed, wrapped in red foil and tied with a white satin ribbon. She didn't have to see the writing on the ribbon to know it came from the specialty candy store in a suburb of Denver...the same store where Stuart had bought candy for her.

Robin took one small step, then another and another, until she stood by the side of her bed. Reaching out a shaky hand, she withdrew the small piece of paper beneath the box. Two words were written on the paper in Stuart's masculine scrawl.

Miss me?

No. Stuart was in prison. He'd been given a twenty-year sentence for setting her house on fire in Denver. He couldn't possibly have been in her home today.

Unless he'd been paroled.

Robin knew it would be useless to call Denver tonight. The Thanksgiving holiday probably changed everyone's normal schedule, and it was past regular working hours. First thing tomorrow, she'd call the authorities in Denver and find out what happened with Stuart.

She looked at the box again. She shivered to think of staying here, not knowing for sure about Stuart, but she refused to let him chase her out of her home.

Robin knelt before her end table. The lower shelf contained several software manuals, novels and scrapbooks. She withdrew a red leather scrapbook and opened it. Instead of seeing dozens of pictures and newspaper clippings that would be in a regular scrapbook, the hollow book held a single item—a .32 caliber semi-automatic.

She removed the gun from its hiding place and clutched it firmly in her hand. If Stuart had been released from prison and decided to come here, she would be ready for him.

Chapter Eight

Brent pushed the last bite of candied yam around on his plate. He remembered when he was a kid and his mom would scold him for not cleaning his plate. There had been many times he simply hadn't been able to eat that last bite.

The fact that his stomach had been churning ever since he left Robin's house probably had a lot to do with his loss of appetite.

He kept seeing her eyes when she'd faced him after he'd looked at her scars. He'd seen anger in those hazel depths, but he'd also seen pain beneath that anger.

He didn't understand why it bothered him so much to know he'd hurt her. He'd always believed that *his* feelings were what mattered, no one else's. As long as he was happy, everything would be cool.

He wasn't happy, and everything most definitely was not cool.

Michelle hadn't exaggerated when she'd called him a jerk. Asshole would probably describe him better.

"Some habits never change, do they?" Colleen asked as she sat in the chair beside him at Jade's dining room table.

Brent chuckled. "That last bite always gets me."

"You cleaned your plate at lunch."

"I had more of an appetite at lunch."

Colleen pushed his hair back from his face. The maternal gesture warmed Brent's heart. His mother had always been a toucher with all her children. A day had never gone by without at least two hugs.

"You've been quiet since you got back from taking Robin home."

He shrugged. The last bite of yam made another circle around his plate on the tip of his fork as his thoughts returned to the pain in Robin's eyes. "Not much to say, I guess."

She laid her hand over his, stopping his movement of the food. "Either eat it or throw it away."

Brent grinned. She'd done the same to him when he was a child. It had become a game with them, him teasing her by playing with his last bite of food. "You realize I do that to aggravate you."

"Yes, but that's enough."

He laid his fork on his plate and leaned back in his chair, his gaze focused on that piece of yam. "Jade told me today you didn't spank me enough when I was a kid."

"I'm sure that's true." She touched his hair again. "Y'all were good kids, most of the time. Usually a stern look from either your father or me was enough."

"Or one of Dad's talks. He never raised his voice, but I knew when he was disappointed in something I'd done."

"Your eyes always gave you away when you were feeling guilty. Like now."

Brent whipped his gaze to his mother. "I'm not feeling guilty about anything."

She smiled tenderly. "I know my children, Brent. What happened?"

He almost confided in her. He didn't understand how he felt, so didn't know what to tell his mother. "It's not important. I'll work it out."

"I'm here if you need me."

He took her hand in both of his. "I know that, Mom. Thanks."

She remained silent for several moments, studying him. Brent suspected she longed to ask more questions. Thankfully, she didn't. "Well, if you're through playing with your food, how about taking me home? Michelle and the guys are going to stay a while longer."

"Sure."

Brent stepped outside while his mother finished her goodbyes. He could hug and kiss cheeks in a minute. His mother took at least five. She always wanted one more hug.

He wouldn't want her to be any different.

Seeing his SUV parked next to Robin's car brought his thoughts right back to her and what happened at her house. They'd been so close to making love...until he'd seen her back. He hadn't planned to freeze the way he had, but he hadn't been able to stop himself. He'd seen burn victims in television specials and pictures, yet never in real life. Robin had told him surgeries and skin grafts could never completely erase all evidence of burns. Her back proved that.

His mother came out of the house and hurried down the porch steps. "Why are you standing in the cold instead of warming up your truck for me?"

Because I'm too wrapped up in thoughts of Robin. "Sorry. I lost my head."

Colleen waited until they were on the main highway before she spoke again. "The holidays always make me think of your father. I think of him every day, but he's especially on my mind on special days like Thanksgiving, Christmas, his birthday, our anniversary."

"Yeah, I think of him then too." Brent glanced at his mother. His father had died twelve years ago. Colleen admitted she had dated several men in that time, but hadn't become seriously involved with anyone. She was only fifty-two and a very nurturing person. She shouldn't be alone the rest of her life. "You ever think about getting married again?"

"I've thought about it. I doubt I'll ever do it."

"Why not?"

"Because I had the love of my life. A person is blessed to have that special love once. Trying to find it twice would be pushing my luck." She shifted on her seat and turned toward him. "What about you?"

"What about me what?"

"Robin is very nice. I like her."

Brent laughed. His mother had never been subtle. "Don't play Cupid, Mom."

"I don't think I'll have to. I think you're already falling for her."

"I am *not* falling for her."

"I saw the way you looked at her today. I also saw the steam coming out of your ears when she talked to Sandro. You were jealous."

Brent had never experienced jealousy. He couldn't say that's what he felt when he watched Robin and Sandro talking, but he definitely hadn't liked how chummy they'd seemed.

"*Do* you like her?" she asked.

He took the exit off the interstate that led to his mother's house. "Well, yeah, I like her. She's intelligent and a nice person."

"And very pretty."

The vision of her scars flashed through his mind. He couldn't see her blonde hair, her hazel eyes, her curvy body. All he could see were those damn scars.

"You don't think she's pretty?" Colleen asked.

"Yeah, she's pretty."

"You don't sound like you mean that."

"I mean it. She *is* pretty. It's just…" He stopped and blew out a breath. He wasn't going to tell his mother something so private about Robin. "I'm not going to get involved with Robin, so you might as well stop pushing right now."

"Why not? And I do *not* push."

Brent snorted out a laugh. "Yeah, right. You've been pushing me to get married ever since I turned twenty."

"And what's wrong with that? I want my children to be happy. Jade is a wonderful woman. I'm so glad she and Zach got married. Michelle is ecstatically happy with Andre and Nathan." She touched his hand on the steering wheel. "I want *all* my children to be happy."

"A person doesn't have to be married to be happy, Mom. I have a great life. I'm happy now."

Even as he said the words to convince his mother, they left a bitter taste in his mouth.

He pulled into Colleen's driveway. She picked up her purse from the floor and grasped the door handle, then looked back at him. "A person doesn't have to be married to be happy, but a person needs love. You may be happy now, but you won't want to be an escort the rest of your life." She laid her hand on his cheek. "You've always been such a perfectionist. I don't know why that is. Your father and I certainly didn't raise you that way. We raised our children to be tolerant of other people and to always look past the outside."

Heat climbed up his neck into his face. He felt like a little boy again, being chastised by his mother.

"Good looks are nice, Brent, but they don't make a person special. It's the heart that makes a person special. Robin is a lovely woman, but you must not think she's lovely enough. She has a good heart. I hope you realize that before you lose any chance with her."

He watched his mother walk to her front door. He waited until she turned on the lights in her house before he backed out of her driveway. *Robin has a good heart.* His mother couldn't possibly know that after spending a mere three hours with her. Yes, she had a great personality, charm, wit, a pretty face and great body.

She just wasn't...perfect.

Twenty minutes later, he sat in Robin's driveway, staring at her front door. He didn't know why he'd driven here. He wasn't even sure he wanted to talk to her. He didn't know what to say, what to do.

"Shit," he muttered.

He'd never been so confused in his life. He should start his vehicle and leave, right now, before she looked out her window and saw him sitting here like some lovesick idiot.

He turned the key in the ignition and put the gearshift into reverse.

* * * * *

Eating seemed like way too much trouble, but her body still demanded nourishment. Robin ignored her growling stomach as long as she could before heading for the kitchen.

She spotted the plate Jade had given her as soon as she opened the refrigerator. Leftovers would be perfect. She removed the foil from the paper platter to see enough to easily feed two people. She placed one-third of the food on a plate for the microwave and replaced Jade's platter in the refrigerator. The ding on the microwave sounded a moment before her doorbell rang.

If Stuart had come back, surely he wouldn't be stupid enough to assume she'd answer the doorbell. Still, she wouldn't take any chances. Slipping her hand in her pants pocket, she wrapped it around her pistol's grip as she walked to the door.

A sensor turned on her porch light when someone stepped up to her front door. She peered through the peephole to see Stuart hadn't returned. Brent stood on her porch.

The independent woman who'd taken care of herself her whole life balked at him coming back after their argument. The frightened woman—scared that the man who'd tried to kill her may be out of prison—rejoiced at seeing him.

She unlocked the deadbolt and opened the door. He stood with his hands in his jacket pockets, the look on his face that of a little boy who'd just been punished.

"May I come in?"

Robin stepped to the side so Brent could enter the house. She checked the doorknob and deadbolt twice to be sure they were locked before she turned to face him.

"Am I disturbing you?" he asked.

She shook her head. "I was about to eat."

"At ten o'clock?"

"I wasn't hungry earlier."

Robin assumed he was here to apologize for his behavior when he saw her scars. From the uncomfortable look on his face, that wouldn't be easy for him. She could make it more difficult, or she could make it easier. "I'm having Jade's leftovers. Would you like some?"

His shoulders relaxed and a hint of a smile touched his lips. "I had some of her leftovers about an hour ago. I'll take coffee, if you have it."

"I don't, but it won't take long to make it. Take off your jacket and let's go to the kitchen."

She waited until he'd hung his jacket on the coat tree, then led the way to her kitchen. He sat at her small table for two, facing her. She could feel him watching her while she prepared the coffee. She wished she could read his thoughts, know exactly how he felt right now.

"Don't let me stop you from eating."

"I won't." Deciding a bit of humor would lighten the mood, she grinned at him over her shoulder. "No one stands between me and food."

His gaze slowly passed over her body. "It doesn't show."

"I like to walk. It burns off the calories." She took her plate from the microwave and set it on the table. "That is, until winter decided to blow in. I don't walk when it's cold."

"It's hard for me to believe you lived in Colorado and Michigan. They're a lot colder than Texas."

"People who live in colder climates are prepared. I wasn't expecting a blast from the North Pole here."

"It'll warm up again in a few days. That's the way it is in Texas."

She crossed to the cabinets for a fork. While she had the silverware drawer open, she slipped her gun out of her pocket and into the drawer. Brent didn't need to know about her pistol, or about Stuart.

After pouring their coffee, she returned to the table. Brent took a sip of his drink while she dug into her meal. He silently watched her as she ate two bites. She'd forked her third piece of turkey when he finally spoke.

"I'm sorry."

Robin lifted her gaze to his. His expression was serious, his eyes sad. Laying her fork on her plate, she sat back in her chair and waited for him to speak again.

"I didn't mean to hurt you."

"I know you didn't."

He set down his mug and also leaned back in his chair. "I can't stop thinking about you. That's never happened to me."

His confession thrilled her at the same time that it saddened her. Brent may be attracted to her, but she doubted if he wanted to be. She suspected he would never settle for anyone other than his "perfect" woman. He might consider her almost perfect. That wouldn't be good enough.

"So what does that mean?" she asked.

"I don't know. I feel like I've been hit in the head with a two-by-four every time I look at you."

"Not exactly a flattering comparison, Brent."

He chuckled. "Sorry. I think in construction terms since I sometimes work with my uncle."

"Your uncle?"

"He builds houses. Zach and I work with him when he needs help."

She glanced at his hands resting on the table. "That's why you have calluses."

He turned his hands over and gazed at his palms. "Yeah." He looked back into her eyes. "How did you know about my calluses?"

"I noticed them when you drove me home today. I watched your hands on the steering wheel."

"Why did you watch my hands?"

Warmth flowed through her as she remembered how she'd imagined his hands on her body. She wondered if those mental images somehow showed on her face when heat flared in Brent's eyes.

"What did you think when you looked at my hands?" he asked, his voice low and husky.

"It doesn't matter."

Robin picked up her plate and carried it to the counter. She wouldn't be able to swallow another bite now, not with the knot in her throat.

She sensed Brent behind her before he touched her. He slid his hands up and down her arms. "I think it matters very much."

He pushed aside her hair and kissed the side of her neck. "Did you wonder how those calluses would feel when I touched you?"

Robin locked her knees to keep them from trembling. His warm breath tickled the hair at her temple. "Please don't."

"Why not? You want me as much as I want you."

"I'm not perfect, Brent."

Turning her in his arms, he tilted up her face and gently kissed her. "Neither am I."

His next kiss was just as gentle, but much more powerful. Brent's mouth moved over hers, his tongue coaxed her lips to part. Robin clutched his waist, then slid her hands up his back. She returned each of his kisses as she learned the shape of his body…the wide shoulders, the broad back, the indentation of his waist, his tight buttocks.

She threw her head back when his mouth coasted over her cheek to the spot beneath her ear that gave her goose bumps. Closing her eyes, she let herself simply *feel* the pleasure coursing through her body. It had been so long since a man had held her, touched her.

Brent's hands drifted over her lower back beneath her sweater. They slid across her stomach and up to her breasts. Robin arched her back, silently telling him she wanted more. She felt her bra strap tighten, then loosen. A moment later, Brent's warm palms cradled her bare breasts.

"My God, these are incredible," he whispered in her ear.

Robin could do no more than whimper. Brent lifted her breasts, squeezed them, pushed them together. Each tug of her nipples sent a zing directly to her clit. Moisture leaked from her channel to dampen her panties.

She released a squeak of surprise when Brent picked her up and set her on the counter. He whipped her sweater over her head and dropped it on the floor. Her bra went next. Naked from the waist up, she sat still while he looked at her.

"Beautiful." Cradling her breasts in his hands, he bent over and kissed each puckered tip. "I could spend hours sucking your nipples."

Robin could spend hours letting him do that. Her nipples were very sensitive and she loved for a man to play with them. She moaned loudly when Brent drew one into his mouth to suckle.

He rubbed his thumbs over the hard tips. "You like all this attention to your nipples, don't you?"

"Don't talk. Suck."

She grasped his head and directed his mouth back to her breast. He obeyed her command, moving from one nipple to the other while he licked, sucked, bit. Holding one breast while he suckled, he wrapped his other arm around her waist and pulled her closer to the edge of the counter. He stepped between her legs, using his thighs to push them farther apart. Robin moaned again when she felt the hard ridge of his cock against her pussy. He shifted from side to side, brushing her clit with each movement.

"Come for me." He kissed her long and deeply. "I want to feel you come."

She moved with him, pumping her mound against his shaft. The orgasm built so quickly, Robin couldn't hold it back. It broke over her like a wave on the beach, making her tremble. She buried her face in Brent's neck and gripped his waist to keep from dissolving into a puddle on the floor.

Soft kisses fell on her neck and shoulder. "Good one?" Brent asked.

"Definitely." She lifted her head and kissed his mouth. "I'm sorry."

Brent's eyebrows drew together. "Why are you sorry?"

"That was selfish of me. You're still wearing all your clothes."

His frown relaxed and he chuckled. "No complaints from me. I'm happy you came." He kissed her again. "Besides, we aren't even close to finished."

The hard cock pressed between her thighs proved that. "So what are you suggesting?"

"I'm suggesting we go to your bedroom. I want you naked beneath me."

Robin wrapped her arms and legs around him, holding him tightly as he walked out of the kitchen and toward her bedroom.

Chapter Nine

The lamps on either side of the bed came on when Robin flipped the wall switch. Brent quickly took in the feminine furnishings before he focused his attention on the bed. His cock was already hard and ready to thrust into Robin's creamy heat. One quick tumble and they'd both be on that bed.

There wouldn't be anything "quick" about tonight. Brent would make sure of that.

He stopped by the side of the bed and let her slide down his body until her feet touched the floor. Apprehension shone in her eyes, along with desire. He pushed her hair behind one ear and caressed her cheek. "Is something wrong?"

He saw her swallow. "It's…been a while for me."

"I'm not in a hurry." He kissed that spot beneath her ear that he'd already learned made her breath hitch. "I like to savor."

Blood surged in his shaft when he heard that sound of surrender. He moved up her neck, dropping gentle, nipping kisses until he reached her mouth. Brent had kissed countless women since he'd shared that first peck with Janie Blackman when he was eight. Most women responded swiftly to his kisses. He'd used that response to get a woman into bed as soon as possible.

He wanted much more with Robin than a fast fuck.

Her mouth was so soft, so giving beneath his. Brent laid one hand over her heart. It pounded beneath his palm. Moving his hand lower, he cradled her breast. He gently squeezed the full globe while moving his thumb over her hard nipple. Her moan urged him to continue, to give her even more.

He would gladly give her whatever she needed.

She tugged his pullover out of his jeans and slid her hands beneath the fabric. It was Brent's turn to moan when she scratched his nipples.

"You don't like scratching?" she asked against his lips.

"*Love* scratching." He proved his words by digging his fingernails into her ass. "And biting." He scraped his teeth across her neck. "And sucking." Placing his mouth over the throbbing pulse in her neck, he sucked hard. "I love everything about sex."

Still holding tightly to her ass, Brent brushed his cock back and forth against her mound. Robin whimpered. She rubbed both thumbs over his nipples, urging them to hardness. Brent loved her touch, but wanted to give her pleasure before he thought about himself. Grabbing the hem of his pullover, he jerked it over his head and dropped it on the floor. He tugged her closer, until her breasts flattened against his chest.

"Wait." She drew back until they no longer touched. "I want to look at you."

Brent stood still while her gaze moved over him. She simply looked at first, then she touched. She glided her hands over his shoulders, across his chest and down his flat stomach to the waistband of his jeans. She loosened the buckle on his belt before looking back into his eyes.

"Don't stop now," he said, his voice raspy.

Her gaze still locked with his, she unsnapped his jeans and slowly lowered the zipper. Brent kissed her neck again as she pulled his briefs away from his body. He waited, breath held, for her to touch him.

He blew out his breath with a groan when she slid her hand inside to wrap around hot, hard flesh. He hunched his hips forward. "Yeah. Touch me."

She gripped his shaft and ran her thumb over the velvety head. He could feel her thumb sliding through the moisture oozing from the slit. He cradled her jaws and drove his tongue deep into her mouth as she spread the moisture over the tip.

The sensation became too much when she started moving her hand up and down his cock. He had to stop her before he wouldn't be able to.

"How about if we get rid of the rest of our clothes?" Brent asked as he pulled her hand out of his shorts. He gently pushed on her shoulders until she sat on the side of the bed. Dropping to his knees, he slipped off her shoes and socks.

Robin looked at Brent's bent head. His thick hair almost brushed his shoulders. It had been the first thing she'd noticed about Brent when she walked into Coopers' Companions. His eyes had been the second, then his chest. She remembered thinking that he must have hair on his chest.

He did, enough to tickle her fingertips as she dragged them across his flesh. Dark blond hair swirled across his chest and arrowed down his stomach. She'd felt the coarse hair at the base of his cock when she had her hand inside his briefs.

She'd also felt that magnificent cock.

Her mouth watered with the desire to taste him. Her fantasy from two nights ago popped into her head. She could take Brent's hands right now and urge him to stand. A quick tug on his briefs and his rod would pop free, ready for her to lick and suck it.

Brent didn't seem to be in any hurry to remove his clothing, or hers. He'd finished massaging her left foot and now moved to her right. It felt so good, Robin had to concentrate to keep her eyes from crossing. She'd never known her feet were an erogenous zone.

"Do you have lotion?" Brent asked.

She nodded.

"I'll give you a full body massage." He nipped the arch of her foot. "After we make love."

A delicious shiver raced up her spine at the thought of his lotion-slick hands on her body. Scooting closer to the edge of the bed, she leaned over and kissed him. He released her foot and cradled her breasts while lips and tongues danced across each other.

He was breathing as heavily as she when Robin lifted her head. "Take off your clothes, Brent."

"Are you going to help me?"

Robin shook her head. "I'm going to watch."

A crooked grin flashed across his mouth. "Why, you little hussy."

"You have something against hussies?"

"Nope. I happen to love them."

Brent stood. He toed off his shoes first, then removed his socks. Robin's breathing became heavier as she waited for him to take off his jeans and briefs. He hooked his thumbs in the sides of his briefs. Underwear and jeans fell to the floor at the same time. He kicked them aside and stood before her, completely nude.

She'd suspected he would be magnificent. Reality topped her suspicion. He didn't have the heavy muscles of a weightlifter, but the build of a man who took care of himself. His legs were well formed and dusted with the same dark blond hair that swirled over his chest and narrowed down his stomach. His cock stood up, thick and long and straight. Moisture seeped from the tip. Robin wiped the moisture with her fingertip and brought it to her mouth.

One taste wasn't enough. Robin grasped the base of his shaft and took the head in her mouth.

"Oh yeah." Brent tunneled his hands into her hair. "That feels really good."

She circled the rim with her tongue, licked down the entire length to his tight balls. His musky, masculine scent filled her nostrils. Robin breathed deeply of that scent before making the return trip back to the head of his cock. Once more, she circled the rim and licked the length. Brent stopped her from making a third trip. He tightened his hold on her head and gently pulled away from her.

"That's enough."

Not ready to stop, Robin gripped the base and slowly milked his rod. "Oh, it isn't nearly enough."

His nostrils flared, his eyes narrowed. "You're a naughty woman, Robin."

"You said you like hussies." She licked off a drop of moisture that leaked from his slit. "Do you like naughty women too?"

He answered her question with a voracious kiss. Robin continued to milk his cock as they kissed. His mouth slid one way, then the other, his tongue diving deeply into her mouth.

She'd never been with a man who kissed as sexy as Brent.

She whimpered when he pulled away from her hand. She still wasn't ready to stop touching him.

"I want you naked," he growled against her mouth.

He pushed on her shoulders until she lay on the bed. Robin lifted her hips when he tugged on the waistband of her slacks. He pulled them off first and dropped them on top of his clothes. She lay before him in nothing but a pair of pale blue bikini panties.

That crooked grin she now associated with Brent tilted up one corner of his mouth. "And here I thought you'd wear a thong."

"Are you disappointed?"

"No." He leaned over and kissed her mound through the nylon. "I'm not disappointed in anything."

He nipped the same spot he'd kissed. Looking into her eyes, he gripped the waistband of her panties with his teeth and tugged. Robin helped by pushing her underwear past her hips. Still holding the elastic with his teeth, Brent pulled them down her legs.

After dropping them on the floor, he leaned over her, his hands on either side of her waist. His gaze swept the entire length of her body. "Much better."

Robin thought she might seriously hurt him if he didn't touch her soon. Her climax in the kitchen had been staggering, but it had happened half an hour ago. Her body demanded another one, and soon.

She wrapped her hand around his cock and spread her legs. "I want you inside me."

Brent shook his head. "If I get inside you now, we'll fuck."

She didn't understand what he meant. "And that would be a problem...why?"

"I don't want to fuck you, Robin. I want to make love to you."

He kissed her...not the intense, passionate kisses of a few minutes ago, but the soft, sweet kisses of a longtime lover. Robin slid her hands up his arms, over his shoulders, into his hair. She clutched the blond strands as his tongue coaxed her lips to part.

The man's kisses could melt a woman's bones. But then, Robin knew he'd had a lot of practice as an escort. He'd probably kissed dozens of women, maybe even hundreds. He'd had sex with just as many.

He wasn't with any of those women now. He was with *her*, his hand cradling her breast as he licked her nipple. His other hand crept between her legs, fingers delving through her creamy folds to circle her clit.

"Mmm, you're nice and wet."

Each pass of his fingertips took her nearer to another orgasm. Robin lifted her hips to get closer to his touch. Just a little more...

"I think you need more than my fingers."

She grabbed his wrist to keep him from moving his hand. "Your fingers are doing fine."

He chuckled, low and wicked. "No, you definitely need more." He dropped to his knees at the side of the bed. Slipping his arms beneath her knees, he dragged her hips right to the edge. "Don't you?"

He spread her labia with his thumbs and licked her...a long, slow stroke the length of her folds. After he did that, Robin wasn't able to talk. She closed her eyes and twisted the bedspread in her fists when he licked her again. His stroke was longer this time, from her anus to her clit.

"Damn, you taste good."

He circled her clit with the tip of his tongue, then darted it inside her channel. Robin almost cried out, the pleasure was so intense. She hooked her hands behind her knees and spread her legs wider to give Brent more room. He licked her pussy over and over, concentrating on her clit and anus. Robin's orgasm drew closer every time he touched her clit.

Kissing wasn't the only thing Brent knew how to do well.

He bit the inside of each thigh, then stood and leaned over her. He rubbed his cock up and down her slit as he kissed her. Robin tasted her own juices on his lips. She wrapped one arm around his neck and held his head while she thrust her tongue into his mouth. Reaching between their bodies, she grabbed his cock. "Condom. Now."

He pulled back from her. "No. Not yet."

She was definitely going to hurt him. Robin released a sound of frustration. "Why not?"

"I want you to come first."

"Coming won't be a problem, believe me."

"Good. I like that."

He kissed her mouth and each nipple before dropping to his knees again. He began to feast on her pussy...licking, sucking, darting his tongue inside her. Robin arched her hips and pushed her mound closer to his mouth. Her orgasm was there, right *there*. She needed *something* to help her get over the top.

He pushed two fingers inside her and pressed up on her G-spot as he suckled her clit. Robin keened when the pleasure swept through her body. The waves flowed through her, one after the other, slowing in intensity until she lay still.

Brent had no idea how many women he'd pleasured. None of them were as beautiful as Robin in the throes of climax.

Locating his jeans on the floor, he drew out his wallet and found a condom. He quickly donned it, then leaned over Robin again.

"Move to the middle of the bed."

She slowly opened her eyes, blinking several times as if to bring him into focus. "Move? Surely you aren't serious."

He chuckled. He liked her sense of humor. "You have a very horny man here who has all kinds of ideas of what to do to you."

"Oh. Well, in that case…" She shifted until she could tuck a pillow beneath her head. Brent followed and stretched out on top of her body. His lips met hers while he entered her with one thrust.

She groaned and arched her back. Brent immediately stilled. He'd forgotten she'd said she hadn't made love in a while. "Did I hurt you?"

"Yes. No. I mean, it's a good hurt."

"I'm sorry." He kissed her softly. "Do you want me to stop?" He wasn't sure how he'd do that when every hormone in his body urged him to pump, but he'd quit before he'd hurt Robin.

"No." She ran her hands up and down his back. "Don't stop. Make love to me."

Brent kissed her as he began to thrust. He heard the catch in Robin's throat, that sexy sound of pleasure. He moved slowly, letting her body adjust to him. She dug her fingernails into his shoulders and threw back her head. The sign of surrender urged him to move faster. Slipping his hands beneath her buttocks, he lifted her hips so he could thrust deeper.

"I love being inside you." He straightened his arms and lifted his torso away from her. He gazed at her breasts, then moved down to where their bodies were joined. He watched his wet cock sliding in and out of her slick channel. Hooking one arm beneath her knee, he raised her leg so she could also see where they were joined. "Look at that."

She did, gripping his shoulders as she watched him thrusting into her. She drew her bottom lip between her teeth.

"It looks good, doesn't it?"

"Yes." Her eyes drifted closed, her head tilted back. "Brent."

"What? What do you need me to do?"

"Just-just keep… Oh, God!"

Her back bowed as she dug her fingernails into his skin. Her nipples beaded, a sheen of sweat covered her skin. Brent pushed his cock all the way inside her. The walls of her pussy milked it, signaling her climax.

She opened her eyes and smiled at him. Brent kissed her forehead, the tip of her nose, her lips. "You're so beautiful when you come."

She tunneled her fingers into his hair. "You didn't."

"Not yet. I'm not through with you."

Her sudden laughter made him smile. "Brent, I've had three orgasms. That's it. No more."

"Never say never." He cradled one breast and thumbed the nipple. "I might have some tricks you haven't seen."

He began to thrust again, slow and steady. He surprised her by rising to his knees, his shaft still inside her. Clasping her wrists, he pulled her up to straddle his lap. He held her ass and continued to pump.

The new position caressed her clit with each movement. Robin was shocked to feel her desire climbing again. That surprise soon turned into pleasure. Brent nibbled and sucked on the pounding pulse in her neck. Robin wrapped her arms around his neck as his thrusts quickened. The pleasure grew, sweeping through her body and stealing her breath. It peaked a moment before Brent's body shuddered.

"Oh *fuck*!" he breathed into her ear. Another tremor passed through him and he tightened his arms around her. "God, that was incredible."

"Yes, it was." She leaned back so she could see his face. "You're an amazing lover."

"*You're* the amazing one."

His eyes were such a stunning blue. Robin traced his mustache with one fingertip, then his full lips. He was so handsome, he stole her breath every time she looked at him.

He playfully nipped the end of her finger. "Wanna try for five?"

Robin burst out laughing while Brent grinned. "Hey, I figured it wouldn't hurt to ask. I'll be happy to do whatever you need to reach that fifth orgasm. And the sixth, and the seventh—"

She placed her fingers over his mouth. "I am completely satisfied."

He removed her hand and kissed her palm. "Good."

He stared into her eyes. Robin wondered if this would turn into "awkward after sex moment" when he lowered her to the bed and kissed her.

"I'll be right back."

She admired his back and buttocks as he walked out of the room. She assumed he planned to use her bathroom to dispose of his condom. She was glad he'd had one with him since she hadn't purchased any in a long time. In his line of work, he would always have to be prepared.

He came back into the bedroom. Climbing on the end of the bed, he crawled between her legs and rested his head on her stomach. Robin touched his head, her fingers sliding through his hair. "You have a thing for tummies?"

He snuggled closer to her, rubbing his face over her stomach the way he would a pillow. "I like tummies." A loud gurgling filled the air. Brent jerked up his head. "Except when they growl in my ear."

Robin's face heated with embarrassment. "Sorry about that."

Brent chuckled. "I think you're hungry."

"I didn't get to eat because *someone* decided to have sex in the kitchen."

He rubbed his chin on her abdomen. "I don't remember hearing any complaints."

"Probably because I didn't make any."

Her stomach gurgled again. "Okay, okay," Brent said, laughter in his voice. "I'll feed you." He kissed the spot he had rubbed with his chin. "Be right back."

"Where are you going?"

"To heat up Jade's leftovers."

"I can do it."

He crawled farther up the bed and kissed her lips. "Let me wait on you, okay?"

She couldn't argue with an offer like that. It had been a long time since a man had waited on her...especially a naked one. Brent didn't bother to put on any clothes before he left the bedroom.

A sudden chill made her shiver. Now that she'd stopped all the physical activity, her body had cooled. She drew up the light quilt from the end of the bed and covered herself. She could hear Brent in the kitchen, opening and closing the refrigerator, opening a cabinet, running the microwave. Those little sounds comforted her. She'd wanted to have someone in her life for a long time. She knew Brent didn't believe in happily-ever-after with one person. Still, she'd enjoy having him in her house and her bed until he decided they were getting too close. As long as she didn't do something stupid like fall in love with him, they could have a really good time together.

The kitchen noises stopped. Robin fluffed the pillow beneath her head and waited for Brent to come back to bed. A few moments later, he walked into the bedroom. He wasn't carrying a plate. Instead, he stopped at the foot of the bed, one hand behind his back. She didn't understand why he had a frown on his face.

"Did you forget the plate?" she asked.

"It's in the microwave. I opened your silverware drawer for forks. I found this."

He held out his hand. Her pistol lay on his palm.

His frown deepened. "Would you like to explain to me what the hell this is?"

Chapter Ten

Brent had never seen a person's face pale so quickly. Guilt filled her eyes before she looked away from him.

"Robin. Why do you have a gun?"

She climbed from the bed and reached for her robe hanging on the footboard's post. "I thought guns were given as christening presents in Texas."

"Right. That ranks up there with every Texan having an oil well in his backyard."

She tied the belt on her robe with a fast yank. "Brent, I'm a single woman. I have a gun for protection."

"You keep it in your silverware drawer?"

He noticed her gaze skittered around the room, but never focused on him. "I'm hungry."

She hurried past him before he could grab her arm to stop her. Blowing out a deep breath, Brent laid the pistol on her dresser. Something wasn't right. Robin had every right to have a gun, but it didn't make sense that she kept it in the kitchen.

Brent tugged on his jeans and pullover and left the bedroom. He entered the kitchen to find Robin sitting at the table. She'd poured fresh coffee for both of them. An empty plate sat in front of her and the other chair. The platter of food sat in the middle of the table.

"There's plenty for both of us if you're hungry."

She still hadn't looked directly into his eyes. If she had nothing to hide, she shouldn't be afraid to look at him.

Sitting at the table, he sipped his coffee while she took what food she wanted from the platter. Once she'd filled her plate, he scooped some food onto his plate. He managed to down two bites before he couldn't swallow anything more. He laid down his fork and sat back in his chair. "Robin."

She froze in the process of stabbing a piece of turkey.

"We spent the last hour making love. It meant a lot to me. If there's something wrong, please tell me."

Slowly, she laid her fork on her plate and looked at him. He could see the indecision in her eyes. She obviously didn't want to confide in him.

"I was checking the pistol to be sure it was loaded when you came. I slipped it in my pocket. When I opened the drawer for a fork, I realized I didn't need to keep carrying the pistol in my pocket, so I laid it in the drawer. End of story."

He didn't believe that was the end of the story any more than he believed he'd win the Miss America contest. "Why were you checking to see if it was loaded?"

"What good is a gun if it isn't loaded?"

"Did you hear a noise? Did someone try to break in? What—"

"Brent, I'm fine. Nothing happened." She nodded toward his plate. "Eat. We can't waste Jade's leftovers. They're too good."

Robin picked up her fork and began eating again. The subject was apparently closed. Not for Brent. He wouldn't push her, but he *would* find out whatever she was hiding.

Following her cue, he went back to his own meal. He wanted her to be comfortable with him. He decided the best way for that to happen would be to change the subject. "I think Jade's dressing is better now than it was at lunch."

"It's incredible. Do you think she'll give me the recipe?"

"You can ask." He ate the last bite of turkey on his plate. "Do you like to cook?"

"I do, but I don't do it very often for just me." She pushed aside her empty plate and picked up her coffee mug. "Do you cook?"

Brent nodded. "I'm not the gourmet cook Zach is, but I'm pretty good." He picked up his own mug. "Breakfast is my specialty."

"Oh, really?" she asked, a hint of a grin turning up her lips.

"I make the best Western omelet you've ever tasted."

"I'll bet you've made omelets for a lot of women."

He drained his mug and set it back on the table. "Actually, no. I don't spend the night with women."

Surprise flashed through her eyes. "Never?"

He shook his head. "I've never spent an entire night with a woman."

"How long have you been an escort?"

"Eight years."

"You've never spent the night with any of your...dates?"

"Nope."

"College? Not then either?"

"Nope."

He could see the doubt in her eyes. He raised one hand, palm toward her. "I swear it's true."

"Why not?"

Brent shrugged. "Escorting is my job. Once the evening is over, I go home to my own bed."

Robin silently stared at him a moment, then stood and gathered up their dishes. Brent followed her with their mugs. He watched her rinse off the plates and stack them in the sink. Her mussed hair fell over her shoulders. Her face was bare of makeup. She looked like she'd just gotten out of bed after being thoroughly loved.

He could see an enticing amount of cleavage through the part in her robe. He hadn't played nearly enough with those full breasts. If he stayed with Robin, he could spend the rest of the night touching them...and her.

Brent suddenly realized he wanted very much to spend the night with Robin.

Moving behind her, he wrapped one arm around her waist. He pulled her robe off one shoulder and kissed her creamy flesh. "I'd like to make that omelet for you tomorrow morning." He kissed her shoulder again. "Any objections to me spending the night?"

Her hands stilled as she turned off the water. "Spend the night?"

"Mmm-hmm."

"You said you don't spend the night with women."

"I don't. Until now." He turned her in his arms. "I want very much to hold you all night and wake up beside you in the morning."

Her smile made her eyes shine. "I'd like that."

Brent helped Robin put away things in the kitchen and turn out the lights. In the bedroom, he slipped out of his clothes as she removed her robe. He crawled beneath the covers with her and tugged her into his arms. Sighing softly, she laid her head on his shoulder. "Good night," he whispered before kissing her forehead.

*****

Stuart watched the lights go off in the bedroom before switching his attention to Brent's SUV in the driveway. He knew for a fact that Brent never spent the night with his dates. Brent had told him that more than once. He fucked their brains out, then went home.

He picked a bad time to change his habits.

Stuart didn't want to hurt Brent. He really didn't. But Brent had crossed the line when he decided to fuck Robin. No man was allowed to touch Robin. She belonged to *him*.

A simple lesson would be good. Stuart didn't have to hurt Brent. He could send a signal first. As long as Brent stayed away from Robin, he could keep on living.

Stuart hadn't seen a car come through the quiet neighborhood in almost an hour. Everyone was in bed, nursing their turkey hangovers. After checking once more for any traffic, he exited his car and made his way across the street to Robin's house.

Smiling broadly, he drew a dagger from inside his boot and knelt beside Brent's vehicle.

* * * * *

Robin awoke the next morning to Brent licking her pussy.

She didn't open her eyes for fear he'd stop. She lay still, absorbing the pleasure from his mouth. He ran his tongue up and down her folds and over her clit. He didn't suckle her clit, he didn't dart his tongue inside her. He simply licked her, over and over.

Soon, lying still was no longer an option for Robin. She lifted her hips to get closer to that wondrous tongue. With all that attention to her clit, her desire grew steadily until it rushed through her body in a staggering climax. Only then did she open her eyes. Brent propped his chin on her tummy, looking at her with smoldering eyes.

"Good morning," he said, his voice low and husky.

"Good morning."

He rose over her. Robin had but a moment to admire his body and see he'd already donned a condom before he kissed her. "Are you sore?"

She was, a little, but she wouldn't let that stop her from making love with Brent. She shook her head.

He spread her legs with his knees and entered her. He moved slowly, his cock sliding inside her channel an inch at a time. Robin stared into his eyes as she met each thrust. He didn't quicken his thrusts, but continued the steady pace that refueled her desire.

His breathing became heavier. He buried his face against her shoulder. Robin felt his body shudder, heard the long moan that came from his throat. She wrapped her arms around his neck and held him while he surrendered to his orgasm.

Long moments passed, moments where she caressed his back and buttocks. She loved the feel of his body on top of hers, his softening cock still nestled inside her. She had no idea how many months it had been since she'd held a man like this after making love.

She'd missed it.

Brent raised his head and kissed her tenderly. "Now that is a great way to start the day."

"See all the early morning sex you've missed by not spending the night with women?"

"The wait was worth it."

He kissed her lips again, then moved down her neck. He dropped kisses on her chest, the top of each breast, both nipples. His shaft slid out of her when he rose to his knees. "Be right back."

Robin enjoyed the view of his ass as he walked out of the bedroom. She stretched her arms over her head and pointed her toes. Delicious little aches she hadn't experienced in months spread throughout her body.

Desire came naturally to a person. Robin knew that, yet had always tried to ignore it. Fear made a person push aside any other emotions. Stuart had told her prison wouldn't keep him from knowing where she was or what she did…or whom she dated. She wasn't ever supposed to forget that she was his, and he'd reclaim her someday.

Her move from Colorado and his twenty-year prison sentence had made her breathe easier. Yet she'd always been reluctant to get involved with a man, worried that somehow Stuart would find out and hurt him. Maybe even kill him.

The way he'd killed Douglas.

Brent sauntered back into the room in all his naked glory. She drew in a sharp breath at the sight of him. She wanted to start nibbling on his toes and work her way up his body.

A smirk lifted his lips as he crawled back on the bed, straddling her on his hands and knees. "That look in your eyes is pretty hot."

"What look?"

"The one that says you like what you see."

She playfully rolled her eyes. "You and your conceit."

His smirk turned into a grin. "It's part of my charm." He settled on top of her, propping up on his elbows. "You have a choice."

"I do?"

"Mmm-hmm. We can shower first, or I can fix the omelets first."

She noticed how he easily slipped that "we" into his comment. She really liked this teasing Brent. "*We* can shower first? As in you and me together?"

"Yeah. You can wash my back. And anything else you might like to wash." He bobbled his eyebrows.

Robin laughed. "All in the name of conserving water, right?"

"Absolutely. I'm a conservative kind of guy."

"Showering works for me, but you'll have to put your dirty clothes back on."

"Nope. I carry a duffle in my SUV. Zach and I play tennis and basketball a lot, so I carry clean clothes for after I shower." He tugged down the covers so her breasts were exposed. Each nipple received a long lick. "I have more condoms in my bag too."

"Mr. Prepared."

"Just like a boy scout."

He rose to his knees and cradled both breasts in his palms. "God, these are beautiful." He began kneading and lifting them while he brushed his thumbs over the nipples. "Round and firm with pink nipples." He looked into her eyes, that silly grin back on his lips. "Did I mention I love pink nipples?"

"That never came up in our conversation."

"I do. Especially when they're hard like this."

He continued to caress them with his thumbs, sending waves of pleasure to her pussy. Robin was about to tell him to stop playing and suck them when she heard the first notes of *The Good, The Bad and The Ugly*.

"That's Zach." Brent didn't want to stop touching Robin, but his brother could be calling about Coopers' Companions business. He quickly kissed each of Robin's nipples, then reached over the side of the bed for his jeans. He pulled his cell phone out of one of the pockets and flipped it open. "Mornin'."

"Good morning. I talked to Skip a few minutes ago. He can work on Robin's car today."

"Hey, that's great." He looked at Robin. "Zach's mechanic can work on your car today."

"Uh, Brent? You're talking to Robin?"

"Yeah. She's right here."

"She's with you?"

"Well, technically *I'm* with *her*. We're at her house."

"It's kinda early for a visit, isn't it?"

"Is that supposed to be a sneaky way to ask me if I spent the night with her?"

"Did you?"

Brent winked at Robin. "Of course not. I don't spend the night with women."

"Well, I'll be damned. You *did* spend the night with her."

He laughed at the shocked tone in his brother's voice. He could picture Zach sitting at his kitchen bar with his mouth hanging open.

"I hope you didn't wear yourself out. I checked the messages at the office a little while ago. Angela Dubois wants to see you tonight."

Brent quickly sobered. He didn't want to see Angela Dubois. Michelle had dubbed the woman The Barracuda. His sister had no idea exactly how much of a barracuda Ms. Dubois could be. Angela liked a bit of pain with her pleasure. Correction—she liked a *lot* of pain with her pleasure.

He looked at Robin, lying there with her hair spread over her pillow and her lovely breasts begging to be kissed. No. He wanted nothing to do with Angela Dubois, not when he could make love with Robin. "Send someone else."

Zach remained silent for several seconds. "I don't think I heard you right."

"You heard me exactly right. I don't want to be Angela's plaything tonight. Send someone else."

"She asked for *you*."

"So tell her I'm sick. Tell her I'm out of town. I don't care what you tell her, but tell her no."

"You've never turned down a date with any woman. This is your job, Brent."

"I remember when you turned down a date to be with Jade."

"That was different. I loved Jade. You aren't in love with Robin." Zach paused a moment. "Are you?"

Brent's stomach tightened to even hear the word "love". Love meant commitment and being with one person forever.

That wasn't for him. It never would be for him. "Just call Angela and tell her I'm not available."

He shut his cell, ending the conversation. Stretching out on his stomach next to Robin, he dropped a kiss on her lips. "Did you decide if you want a shower or breakfast first?"

"Do you have to work tonight?"

"No. I don't have to do anything but be with you. So, shower or breakfast?"

She ran one fingertip over his mustache. "I think we should have breakfast first to rebuild our strength. Then we should make love again so we'll need that shower."

Brent smiled. "I like the way you think."

Chapter Eleven

ೲ

Robin scooped up the last bite of her omelet on her fork. She'd eaten slowly, wanting to savor every delicious morsel. Brent hadn't exaggerated when he'd said he knew how to make a Western omelet. It had been lacking green pepper since she didn't have any, but he made up for that with extra onion and more spices.

Brent refilled their coffee mugs. "Did you have enough?"

"More than enough. It was wonderful, Brent."

"Thanks." He replaced the carafe on the coffeemaker's warmer and returned to the table. "I'd brag, but that's so unbecoming."

He grinned while Robin laughed. Holding her mug with both hands, she propped her elbows on the table. "So you're a great cook and an incredible lover. What else do you do well?"

"I'm a good carpenter. I enjoy working with my uncle. He not only builds houses, but he builds furniture too. His woodwork is amazing. He built Zach and Jade's dining room table and chairs as a wedding present."

Robin caught herself before her mouth dropped open. "Your uncle *made* that beautiful table and chairs?"

He nodded. "Pretty good, huh?"

She could see the pride in Brent's eyes. "Good doesn't begin to describe it. Does he build furniture on order?"

"He does, but be prepared to fork over a lot. He isn't cheap."

"I wouldn't expect something well built to be cheap." She sipped her coffee and set the mug back on the table. "I want a custom-made desk someday, one with lots of drawers and cubbyholes and a huge top so I can spread out papers and still have room to work."

"He'd build one for you, but you can't be in a hurry. He refuses to rush or cut corners, in his furniture or his houses."

"He probably has a waiting list, huh?"

"A long one."

"That's okay. I'm not ready for the desk yet anyway. I have to find a house first."

"Did you ever think of building one?"

Robin couldn't say she'd ever seriously thought about that. She assumed she'd find a house through a real estate agent. She shook her head.

He pushed his mug aside and leaned forward, resting his arms on the table. "I'll bet you have the exact house in your head that you want. And I'll also bet I can guess what it looks like."

He was entirely too smug with his thinking that he knew what she wanted in a home. Playing along with him would be a good way to knock that smirk off his face. She leaned forward too, copying his position. "So what do I want in a house?"

He rubbed his chin, as if in deep concentration. "Not brick. You want wood so it'll blend in with all the trees surrounding it. Your bedroom has a large bathroom attached with a sunken tub and a shower big enough for two people. A guest room that isn't too big, but comfortable for any guest who may stay with you. An office with your big desk and large windows to let in the natural light. In fact, you'll have large windows all over the house. A huge kitchen since you like to cook. Lots of cabinets made of...ash, I think. That's a nice wood for cabinets. A center island in the kitchen with a butcher block top. Or maybe marble. A rounded archway will lead from the living room into the dining room. You'll have very few paintings on the walls. Instead, you like silk flowers and metalwork. Carpeting in the living room and your bedroom, wood floors through the rest of the house. Ceramic tile in the entryway. An off-white paint on the walls, or a very light neutral color. Wallpaper halfway up the wall in the dining room." He picked up his mug and sipped his coffee. "How did I do?"

Robin's mouth slackened. It was as if he'd gone inside her head and seen the exact house she longed to have. "You did very well. How do you know all that?"

"Because I helped build it. I described Michelle's house."

"You bum." She tossed her napkin at him. Laughing, he ducked so it passed him and landed on the floor. "That wasn't fair."

"I never promised to play fair. And didn't I get it right? I knew you'd like the same type of house as Michelle."

"And how did you know that?"

His smirk faded and his eyes heated. "Because you're both very feminine. And lovely."

She watched his gaze drop to her breasts. They were covered by her robe, but she suspected he was remembering the way they'd looked a short time ago when she and Brent were in bed.

It amazed her how a simple look from him could affect her so much.

"So…" He looked back into her eyes. "Is it shower time?"

"I thought…" Her voice sounded breathless. Robin swallowed and tried again. "I thought we agreed to make love before our shower."

"I think rubbing soap all over your body is great foreplay. What do you think?"

She thought he had an excellent idea. "I'll clean up in here while you get your duffle."

He winked at her, then rose and left the kitchen.

Robin barely had time to clean off the table when she heard the front door slam shut. She hurried out of the kitchen and met a scowling Brent in the dining room.

"*God damn it!*" he roared.

"What's wrong?"

"Some bastard kids slashed my tires." He threw his duffle on the floor. "They couldn't be happy with ruining one. They slashed all four of them!"

A cold chill skittered down her spine. There was a very good possibility it hadn't been kids, but Stuart.

"I have a car," Brent said, "so I won't be stranded."

"But replacing four tires isn't cheap."

"No, and it's damn inconvenient." Placing his hands on his hips, he looked down at the floor and blew out a breath. "Shit."

Tell him about Stuart.

Robin crossed her arms over her stomach. She couldn't get Brent involved in her personal life. It might have been kids who'd slashed his tires rather than Stuart. There was no reason for her to tell him about Stuart's threats seven years ago.

She wasn't under any illusion that her relationship with Brent was based on anything more than sex. He wasn't the type of man who became involved with one woman. She wasn't the type of woman who wanted more than one man in her life, or her bed.

Stalemate.

Brent dug his cell phone out of his jeans pocket. "I'll call Zach and ask him to come get us. He can run us by my condo so I can get my car. Then we can check on the progress of yours."

"Okay."

He cradled her cheek. "I'm sorry. I wanted our day to be different than this." He tilted up her chin and kissed her softly.

"Why don't you get your shower? I'll take care of the kitchen for you after I call Zach."

"Thanks."

Robin waited until Brent went into the kitchen before she turned. She made it two steps when her cell phone rang. Crossing to the table, she found it buried beneath a stack of papers and flipped it open. "Hello?"

"Hi, Robin, it's Michelle Cooper."

"Hi, Michelle."

"I know it's technically a holiday, but I have the whole day free. Andre and Nathan left a few minutes ago to show Sandro around the area. I have no idea when they'll be back. Do you want to get together and work on the website?"

Robin glanced toward the kitchen. She could hear Brent's muted voice, but couldn't make out his words. He'd acted like he really wanted to help her with the website. She wondered if he'd be disappointed when she went back to working with Michelle.

She doubted that. She was sure Brent had plenty to do to keep busy without working with her. "Sure."

"I know you're without a car. Shall I pick you up?"

"No, that's okay. I'll get a ride to your office."

"Okay. It's a little after ten. Do you want to meet about eleven-thirty?"

"That works for me."

"See you later. Bye."

She laid the phone back on the table and headed for the bathroom.

* * * * *

Brent closed the dishwasher and glanced at the clock on the microwave. Zach wouldn't be here for at least thirty minutes. He should tell Robin so she'd know how much time she had to shower and dress.

He could hear the water running as he walked toward the bathroom. The door was ajar. Brent pushed it open and stepped into the steamy room.

Robin stood behind the shower curtain in the bathtub...the *clear* shower curtain. He could see every curve, every drop of water that flowed over her skin.

Clear shower curtain plus wet, naked Robin equaled instant hard-on.

He didn't think. He didn't plan. He acted.

Brent toed off his shoes while he tugged his pullover over his head. His jeans fell in a heap to the floor. Naked, he pulled back the shower curtain and stepped into the tub.

Robin stood with her head tilted back and her eyes closed while she rinsed the shampoo from her hair. It gave Brent time to leisurely gaze at her body. Full breasts, flat stomach, rounded hips, long legs. Even her feet were beautiful.

He stared at the blonde curls on her mound. He wanted to drop to his knees right now, spread her legs and lick all the cream flowing from her pussy.

When he raised his gaze back to her face, she was looking at his cock. He stepped closer and cradled her face in his hands. She raised her eyes. The hazel depths appeared luminous with desire.

The warm water pelted his head and shoulders as he kissed her. She wrapped her arms around his waist and leaned against him. He could feel her pebbled nipples against his chest, her mound cushioning his cock. A low moan came from her throat, proof she felt desire as strongly as he.

"You're so beautiful, Robin." He kissed each eyelid, her nose, her mouth again. "I need to be inside you."

"Yes." She tightened her arms around him. "Brent, yes. Please."

He turned her so her back touched the wall. Slipping his arms beneath her knees, he lifted and spread her legs wide. There was no build-up, no soft caresses and sweet words. This would be raw and fast fucking. With one thrust, he entered her.

Brent alternated between devouring her mouth and sucking her nipples as he pumped into her creamy channel. Her heart thumped rapidly. Her breathing sounded raspy. The sharp bite of her fingernails in his back urged him to thrust deeper. He shifted his body so he could spread her legs farther apart. She gasped, then moaned.

Brent's balls tightened when the walls of her pussy squeezed his cock. His own orgasm snaked down his spine to grab his rod. He continued to thrust until the last flicker of his climax died.

Slowly, Brent lowered Robin's legs until she could stand. Her knees buckled. He wrapped his arms around her and held her until she steadied.

"You okay?" he whispered against her temple.

"Yeah. I think." She released a shaky laugh. "My legs are weak."

"Mine are too. I guess that means we'll have to hold each other tighter."

"I'd like that, but isn't your brother on his way here?"

Brent had forgotten all about Zach. One look at Robin's body and all other thoughts had flown out of his mind. "Yeah, in about twenty minutes."

"I'll get dressed while you finish your shower."

He stopped her before she could push aside the shower curtain to step out of the tub. Robin looked back at him, a question in her eyes. Instead of speaking, he leaned forward and kissed her gently. She smiled at him.

A pressure formed in the middle of Brent's chest. It didn't hurt, but was different than anything he'd ever experienced. It made him want to draw Robin close again and never let her go.

She moved away from him before he got the chance to touch her. Brent decided that was a good thing. He didn't understand that pressure and wasn't sure if he liked it.

Stepping beneath the spray, Brent picked up the bottle of liquid soap and Robin's washcloth. His mind wandered with various thoughts of Coopers' Companions, buying new tires, Michelle's upcoming birthday and what kind of gift he should get her, until he ran the soapy washcloth over his cock. Instantly, his thoughts turned to sex with Robin a few minutes ago…sex where he hadn't worn a condom.

Shit!

Brent had always been careful since his first escort job. Wearing a condom was as automatic to him as breathing. All the escorts had regular physicals and took excellent care of themselves. Coopers' Companions' rules clearly stated that it was up to the escort if the evening continued in his client's bedroom. Brent had sex only with women he carefully chose. He didn't believe in taking chances with his health, or on getting a woman pregnant.

Shit!

Pregnant. Now there was a scary thought. While his mother would be ecstatic to become a grandmother, Brent didn't see himself as father material…especially when a child wasn't planned.

Panicking would be stupid. Robin had already said she hadn't been intimate with a man in a long time, so he didn't have to worry about disease. He simply had to ask her if she used birth control. Easy.

The sound of the hair dryer broke into his thoughts. Brent rinsed the soap from his body, turned off the water and threw back the shower curtain. Robin was bent at the waist, running her fingers through her hair as she used the dryer.

Here in the bright light of the bathroom, he could clearly see the scars on her back.

The automatic tensing he normally experienced when he encountered someone with a physical imperfection didn't happen. His stomach didn't churn, he didn't look away in disgust. Instead, he shifted his attention to Robin's long waterfall of hair and thought of how he wanted to bury his hands in it while he kissed her senseless.

What's happening to me?

She straightened and caught him watching her. She turned off the hair dryer. "Everything okay?"

"Yeah." He reached for the towel she had thoughtfully laid on the toilet lid for him. His hand shook. He clenched it into a fist to stop the shaking before he picked up the towel. "Just wanted to give you plenty of time to do whatever it is you women do in the bathroom."

She grinned. "We all have a secret ritual."

"I believe that. I always had to wait for Michelle to clear out when we were growing up. Thank God I have only one sister."

Robin gave him a quick kiss. "The bathroom is yours. I'll get dressed."

Once again, he took her arm before she could move away from him. "Robin. I need to ask you something."

"Can it wait until I get dressed? Your brother will be here soon. It's too cold to answer the door in my birthday suit."

"Sure," he said, chuckling at her joke.

He watched her leave the room, his gaze focused on that amazing ass. He hadn't touched it nearly enough, or done all the things he wanted to do to it.

He'd broken every rule he'd set for himself as far as sex and women were concerned. He didn't date a woman two nights in a row. He rarely dated a woman twice, period, yet he was thinking about spending a second night with Robin.

She had turned his world completely upside down.
Now it was time to panic.

* * * * *

Brent chatted with his brother as Zach drove, but Robin sensed something bothering him. He'd grown quiet after their shower. She'd assumed he'd join her in the bedroom to dress. It had surprised her to see him walk into the bedroom already fully dressed. He'd stayed long enough to tell her Zach had pulled into the driveway, but she should take her time getting ready. He'd pour his brother a cup of coffee while they waited for her.

She never liked for *anyone* to wait on her, so she'd hurried through a quick makeup job and pulled her hair back into a ponytail. She'd climbed into the backseat of Zach's car so Brent could sit in the front with his brother. It would give the two men time to plan what to do about Brent's SUV, plus give her the opportunity to watch Brent.

Watching Brent certainly wasn't a hardship. She thought about when he'd taken off his shirt last night. One look at his body proved he took care of himself. Dark blond hair spread over his muscular chest and narrowed down his stomach. His shoulders were wide, his stomach flat. Robin had her own physical problems so placed little importance on looks, yet couldn't help but admire such a handsome man.

Right now, she could feel that handsome man slipping away from her.

Robin looked at her hands clasped in her lap. She shouldn't be surprised. While sex with Brent had been the most powerful she'd ever experienced, it was probably no big deal to him. He was used to women coming apart in his arms. He'd wanted her, he'd had her, and now he didn't need her anymore.

She'd finally found a man who was charming, funny, a delight to be with, besides making her toes curl in bed. She'd be lying to herself if she said it didn't hurt to know what she'd had with Brent was a one-time thing.

Robin gathered up her laptop case and purse when Zach pulled into Coopers' Companions. She had a job to do and she'd do it, despite any developing feelings she had for Brent. Those feelings had to be pushed aside right now.

Zach turned and laid his arm across the seat. "I'm going to take Brent tire shopping. Michelle is here, so the door will be open."

"Okay."

He winked at her. "See you later."

Robin climbed out of the car and walked toward the front door. She didn't look at Brent again.

Chapter Twelve

The smell of cookies lured Robin toward the kitchen. She found Michelle there, removing a tray of what looked like chocolate chip cookies from the oven. "Hi."

Michelle smiled at her over her shoulder. "Hi!"

"Zach told me I could just walk in."

"Sure, no problem." She pushed a button on the stove to turn off the oven. "I ate a late brunch, so decided it would be a great time for cookies. How about you?"

"Any time is a great time for cookies."

Michelle grinned. "I knew I liked you."

Robin slid onto one of the stools at the bar and watched Michelle transfer the cookies onto a plate. "They smell wonderful."

"I'd like to take the credit for making them, but I'm a lousy cook. Nathan mixed up the dough for me. All I have to do is bake them. As long as I set the timer, I won't burn them." She set the plate on the counter in front of Robin. "Speaking of Nathan, what did you think of his pictures?"

"They're fabulous. He's a very talented photographer."

"I think so too."

Pride clearly shone in Michelle's eyes. And love. She obviously cared very much for Nathan, and Andre. Robin had seen that same look of love in Michelle's eyes at Thanksgiving when she gazed at the handsome Italian.

"Coffee?" Michelle asked, holding up the carafe.

"Please."

Picking up a cookie, Robin bit into the soft, warm treat. The melted chocolate slid over her tongue and made her taste buds do a happy dance. "Delicious."

"Thanks. I'm lucky that both my guys are good in the kitchen. Andre is the main cook and Nathan is the baker. Well, Nathan's learning to be the baker. He likes making desserts a lot more than meals. I'm content to clean up the kitchen when they're done."

She'd given Robin the perfect opportunity to ask about Michelle's relationship with two men. She didn't want to pry, but she couldn't help her curiosity.

Michelle took two thick mugs out of the cabinet and filled them with coffee. "I can see the question in your eyes. Go ahead and ask."

"It's none of my business."

"But you want to know." After setting one mug in front of Robin, Michelle leaned on the bar on her forearms. "I never ever thought about falling in love with two men. I didn't think it was even possible. I promise you, it's possible. I love both of them with all my heart." A hint of mischief filled her eyes. "And yes, it's wild in bed."

Robin laughed. "I wasn't going to ask."

"But you wanted to."

"Yes, I did."

"I know it's an unusual situation, but it works for us."

"That's what matters."

Michelle straightened and picked up her mug and the plate of cookies. "Let's go in the living room and chat a while. We can start working in an hour or so."

Robin was hoping she'd have the chance to get to know Michelle better. This was the perfect opportunity. "Lead the way."

* * * * *

Brent rubbed the area between his eyes. His head pounded. Buying four tires and making arrangements for them to be put on his SUV had made him angry all over again. He'd like to wring the necks of the little bastards who thought destruction was fun. He and Zach had been far from perfect when they were kids, but they'd never willfully destroyed something that belonged to someone else.

"You okay?" Zach asked.

"Hell, no. I'm pissed."

"Can't blame you for that." He checked the traffic behind him and pulled into the right lane. "I say it's time for a beer at First and Ten. I'm buying. What do you say?"

"I say that's a great idea."

Five minutes later, Zach pulled into the parking lot of the sports bar. There were a number of vehicles there, more than Brent expected to see on a day when the Cowboys weren't playing. "It's busy today," he said as he and Zach stepped through the entrance.

"Probably all the husbands whose wives are shopping."

"I forgot about that. Did Jade go?"

"Oh yeah. Breanna spent the night so she and Jade could leave the house at six-thirty." He led the way to a table in the corner. "She hits the snooze button twice any other time, but she jumped out of bed when the alarm rang this morning."

"She's a dedicated shopper."

"I told her to have fun, but try not to break the credit card."

Nikki strolled up to their table, order pad in hand. "Hi, Brent, Zach. Your usual?"

"Yeah." Zach looked at Brent. "You hungry?"

"I could eat."

He turned back to Nikki. "Two ribeye sandwiches and fries to go with those beers."

She noted their order on her pad and flashed both of them a bright smile. "You got it."

Brent gazed at the large TV over the bar in time to see one of the soccer teams make a goal. He didn't think soccer was played in November, so the game must be a rerun.

"Are you ever going to tell me what happened with you and Robin?"

It surprised Brent that Zach had waited this long to bring up the subject of Robin. He kept watching the soccer game as he answered his brother's question. "We fucked."

As soon as those two words were out of his mouth, Brent regretted saying them. He and Robin hadn't fucked, at least not last night. This morning in the shower had been hot and wild, but they'd made love last night.

"You know, it wouldn't kill you to be less crude," Zach said, the annoyance clear in his tone.

Brent faced his brother. Zach had always been there for him, ready to listen to whatever Brent wanted to say. He had no doubt today would be the same.

"I felt the tension between y'all as soon as she came near you. You didn't even speak to her in the car. That's a hell of a way to treat her after using her last night."

"I didn't use her. We both wanted to make love."

Zach leaned back in his chair. "So you've gone from fucking to making love?"

Brent remained silent while Nikki placed their mugs of beer on the table. He took a sip of the brew while waiting until she was far enough away that she couldn't hear him. "I hurt Robin yesterday. I went back last night to apologize and… Well, things progressed from there."

"You spent the night with her."

Brent nodded.

"So what was with the cold shoulder this morning? You still hung up on her scars?"

"No. That's the weird thing. I saw her back clearly this morning in the bathroom. I didn't get that weird tighten-my-gut feeling I usually get when I see something like that. All I could think about was kissing her."

Brent scowled when he saw the smirk on Zach's lips. "Get that damn smirk off your mouth."

"Hell no. I'm enjoying this. The eternal bachelor, the man who would never settle for almost perfection, has fallen for a woman who isn't physically perfect."

"I haven't fallen for her. It was one night. That's it."

"Uh-huh."

Brent didn't get the chance to fire back at Zach for Trey approached their table. "Hey, guys." He pulled a chair over from another table. Turning it backward, it straddled it and rested his arms on the back. "What's up?"

"I'm buying my brother lunch," Zach said. "He's had a shitty morning."

"Oh?" Trey looked at Brent. "What happened?"

"Some idiot kids slashed all my tires last night."

Trey winced. "Damn. That put a dent in your wallet."

"It isn't the cost that bothers me. It's the destruction and lack of respect for someone else's property."

"Yeah, that sucks. Did it happen at your condo?"

"No." Brent hesitated a moment, not wanting to give out any private information about Robin, not even to a friend. "It happened somewhere else."

"At a lady's house," Zach said, grinning.

"Oh yeah?" Trey also grinned while leaning forward. "Tell me more."

Now he had two men teasing him, which Brent didn't need. "There's nothing to tell. It was a one-time thing. No repeats."

"Hey, Trey." One of the waitresses held up the phone receiver when he glanced her way. "Phone call."

"Thanks." He looked back at the two brothers, the grin still on his lips. "Don't leave until I hear the whole story."

"You've heard it," Brent said. "Goodbye."

Laughing, Trey walked away as Nikki arrived with their food. Brent dug right into his sandwich to avoid talking to his brother.

That worked for the length of time it took Zach to pour ketchup on his plate. "I checked email and voice mail again before I picked up you and Robin. All the guys have checked in about the pictures except for Jim and Rubin."

"That's weird about Jim. He's always the first escort to respond to our group messages."

Zach swirled a French fry through the dollop of ketchup on his plate. "He did ask for this weekend off. Maybe he's out of town for the holiday."

"He still checks in, even when he's gone. He loves sending email on that fancy cell phone."

"That's true." Zach ate his fry before speaking again. "Pierce agreed to see Angela tonight."

Brent hadn't given Angela Dubois another thought. He had other things on his mind than the spoiled rich girl. "Good."

"You gonna tell me why you were so adamant about not seeing her tonight?"

"I was with Robin when you called. I couldn't agree to go out with another woman so soon after being with her."

"That's never bothered you. I know of weeks when you saw four women over four nights."

"That was different."

"How?"

Brent didn't know. He only knew everything with Robin was different than what he'd ever experienced with another woman. "It just is."

That smirk curved Zach's lips again. Brent seriously thought about knocking it off with his fist. "Eat your sandwich before I steal it."

"Yep, you're a goner. I can't wait to tell Michelle."

Brent slammed his empty mug on the table. "God damn it, Zach, knock it off. I'm not a goner. I'm not in love with Robin."

"Maybe not yet, but you're on the way."

"Shit. I can't believe I'm getting this abuse from you."

"I haven't begun to abuse you."

The laughter in Zach's voice grated on Brent. He clenched his teeth while Zach pulled money from his wallet to cover the bill. He didn't need his brother telling him how he felt. He didn't love Robin. There was no way he'd let himself fall in love. He wanted a good time with a woman. That was enough.

* * * * *

Robin crossed her arms over her stomach and tried to control her laughter. Her sides actually ached from laughing so hard. Michelle had a wicked sense of humor. She turned everything Robin said into something naughty.

"What?" Michelle asked with an innocent expression on her face, but amusement in her eyes.

"You turn everything I say into sex."

"Everything you say has to do with sex."

"How does working on a website turn into sex?"

"Working at it, positioning, putting things in the right place…"

"You're really pushing it, Michelle."

"See, there you go again. Pushing it could be—"

"I don't need to know what it could be." She wiped the tears from the corners of her eyes. "I haven't laughed so hard in months."

"Then you needed it."

"Yes, I did. But maybe it's time to get to work."

"Okay. You want a refill on your coffee?"

"Please."

Michelle stood and gathered up their dishes. "I'll get our refills while you set up your laptop."

Robin moved to the large desk and removed her laptop from the case. She pressed the power button and organized her other items while waiting for it to boot. She'd printed out the pages she'd done so far of Coopers' Companions' site, plus made two mock-ups of different layouts so Michelle could pick her favorite.

Michelle set Robin's mug next to the laptop and took the second chair. Rolling the chair closer to Robin, Michelle peered at the screen. "Whatcha got?"

"Take a look at those printouts while I open the program."

Michelle flipped through the pages, her smile growing every time she flipped a page. "Robin, these are wonderful! I love what you've done."

"I made a couple of mock-ups in case you want something different."

"No, no, this is perfect. It's exactly what I want. It's like you went inside my head and read my mind."

"There's a scary thought."

Michelle grinned. "True." She motioned toward Robin's computer. "I want to see it onscreen."

"Okay."

Robin opened her website program and scrolled through the folders until she found the one for Coopers' Companions.

She clicked on the file "index" and waited to see the opening page of the site.

Instead of the page she'd worked so hard to make perfect, she saw a black background with white letters in a font that looked like dripping blood.

You're mine, Robin. Don't ever forget that.
I'll come for you soon.

"No," Robin whispered. "No."

Staring at the screen, she rolled her chair back to get away from the message until the wall stopped her retreat. The message seemed to get bigger the farther away she moved from it. Her throat closed off, making it difficult for her to breathe.

Michelle grabbed her arm and shook it hard. "Robin! What happened? What is that?"

"Stuart," she said, her voice breaking.

She saw movement out of the corner of her eye, but continued to stare at the screen. He must have done this when he broke into her house yesterday. But she'd hidden her computer in her closet. He couldn't possibly have found it.

"Come here, quick," Michelle called out.

The anxious tone to Michelle's voice jerked Robin out of her trance. She looked away from the computer to see Zach and Brent hurry into the room.

"What's wrong?" Zach demanded.

"I'm not sure. Robin saw this message on her computer and freaked."

Brent squatted next to Robin's chair and looked at the screen. His gaze whipped back to Robin's face. Rage filled his eyes. "What the hell is this?"

"It-it's Stuart." Her voice still sounded raspy. She swallowed hard.

"Who is Stuart?"

"He-he's found me." Tears filled her eyes and she began to shake. "He's su-supposed to be in prison, but he's h-here."

"Michelle," Zach said calmly, "please get Robin a glass of water."

"Sure." Michelle lightly touched Robin's shoulder as she passed her. "Be right back."

Brent had never seen so much fear in a person's eyes. He had no idea who this Stuart was, but Robin was obviously terrified of him. He stood and took Robin's hands. "Let's go to the couch, okay? You'll be more comfortable."

She let him lead her, which he knew was out of character for Robin. He hadn't known her long, but long enough to know she was an independent woman who didn't let anyone tell her what to do.

He sat down on the couch and tugged Robin down beside him. Zach sat on the coffee table in front of her. Michelle came back in the room and took the couch on the other side of Robin. She pressed the glass of water into Robin's hands. "Here."

Brent could see Robin's hands shaking as she tried to raise the glass to her lips. He laid his hands over hers to help. She shot him a grateful look and took a small sip of water.

"Better?" he asked.

Robin nodded.

Taking the glass from her, Brent set it on the coffee table. This was way out of his comfort zone. He didn't take on women's problems. Hell, he didn't take on *anyone's* problems. He'd always been the good-time guy, the one who only worried about himself. He glanced at Zach, silently asking for help.

Zach seemed to understand what Brent wanted. He clasped his hands together between his spread knees. "Robin, take a deep breath and tell us what happened."

She inhaled deeply and let her breath out slowly. "That message is from Stuart Holden."

"Who is Stuart Holden?"

"A former boyfriend. We went together eight years ago. When he became too possessive, I broke off with him. He didn't accept that."

She stopped. Brent waited, but she remained silent. He slid his arm along the back of the couch and inched closer to her, offering her his support.

Zach lightly touched her knee. "What happened then?"

"He-he set fire to my house while I was in it."

Michelle gasped. "Oh, my God!"

Brent had been angry many times in his life. None of those times compared to this. He wanted to hunt down this Stuart, lock the son of a bitch inside a house and see how he liked it when Brent set fire to it.

"You said he's supposed to be in prison," Zach said.

"I saw him outside my house shortly before the fire started. I testified against him. My testimony and evidence the police found in his pickup was enough for the jury to convict him. He was found guilty and sentenced to twenty years in prison. That was seven years ago. He shouldn't be out yet!"

"Maybe he shouldn't be out, but looks like he is. Do you have any idea how he got that message on your computer?"

She glanced at Brent and bit her bottom lip. The tightening in his gut told him he wouldn't like what she was about to say. "He was in my house yesterday."

"What!" Brent roared. "He was in your *house* and you didn't *tell* me?"

"Brent, let her talk," Zach said. "Robin, how do you know he was in your house?"

"There was a specialty candy store outside of Denver. Stuart always bought candy for me there. It came in a red box tied with a white ribbon. I found a box of the candy on my bed last night with a note from Stuart. I recognized his handwriting."

"What did the note say?"

"Miss me, with a question mark."

Brent couldn't sit still any longer. Surging to his feet, he took several steps away from the group before whirling to face Robin. "Why the *hell* didn't you tell me this last night?"

"Because I didn't want to involve you!"

"Well, guess what? I *am* involved."

Zach stood and grabbed his brother's arm. "Calm down."

Brent jerked his arm away from Zach. "Don't tell me to calm down. I'm mad as hell right now."

"I know that, but we need to help Robin. One of your tantrums isn't going to help her."

Brent clenched his fists. He needed to hit someone…preferably the bastard who had hurt Robin. Knowing Zach was right about helping Robin, Brent slowly unclenched his fists and nodded.

Zach returned to his place on the coffee table. "We have a good friend who's a detective with the Fort Worth police department. How about if I call him and have him come over and talk to you?"

Robin nodded.

Michelle touched Robin's arm. "You shouldn't go back to your house alone. You're welcome to stay at my house."

"Or with Jade and me. We have plenty of room."

"No," Brent said firmly. "Robin is staying with me."

Chapter Thirteen

Brent didn't realize how loud silence could be. Everyone stared at him after his statement, yet no one spoke. Michelle finally broke the silence.

"You want Robin to stay with you?"

"Yeah."

"But you don't take women home with you. Ever."

Brent frowned at his sister. "This isn't a date, Michelle. Robin needs protection."

The spark and independence Brent was used to seeing in Robin's eyes returned. She stood and faced him. "I don't need protection. I'm not a little girl."

"I know you aren't a little girl, but you can't seriously think you should go back to your house alone."

"I can take care of myself."

"How? With that pistol in your silverware drawer?"

The light bulb went off in his head as soon as he asked that question. "That's why you had your pistol out yesterday. You saw that note from Holden and carried your gun in case he came back."

Crossing her arms over her stomach, she lowered her head.

"Jesus, Robin, do you realize how stupid that is?"

Her eyes blazed with anger when she looked back at him. "Do *not* call me stupid."

"I didn't call you stupid. I said—"

"For your information, I have a permit for that gun and I'm an excellent shot."

"That's beside the point!"

"I've been taking care of myself my whole life."

Brent pointed toward the chair at the desk where Robin had sat when she got the message from Stuart. "You were shaking when I came in. You're terrified of Holden."

"Wouldn't you be terrified of someone who tried to kill you and did kill someone you cared about?"

Complete silence again. Brent stared at Robin as her eyes widened and her face paled. "What did you say?"

Zach stood and reached for the cell phone at his hip. "I'd better call Stone."

"I'll make fresh coffee," Michelle said. She rose and followed Zach out of the room.

Once his siblings left, Brent stepped closer to Robin. He didn't want to yell at her. He'd done that enough today. "What did you mean by Holden killing someone you care about?"

Sighing heavily, Robin flopped back on the couch. "I don't know for sure that Stuart killed Douglas, but I believe he did."

Brent sat beside her. "Who's Douglas?"

"I started dating him after I broke up with Stuart, or I guess I should say after I *tried* to break up with him." She clasped her hands together in her lap. "Stuart refused to leave me alone. He kept calling and emailing, telling me I belonged to him and he'd never let me go."

She rubbed her forehead, as if she were trying to clear her thoughts. Brent noticed her hand was trembling again.

"I was in the hospital after the fire. A friend of mine visited and told me Douglas was killed in a car accident. I always wondered if, somehow, Stuart had caused the accident."

"Didn't the police investigate the accident?"

Robin nodded. "The sheriff's department did. There were skid marks from Douglas' tires. The sheriff decided he'd swerved to miss a deer or other animal. That made sense. It happened on a road in the woods and there were a lot of deer in the area."

"But you don't believe it."

"No. Stuart had threatened to kill any man I dated. I believe he caused the accident."

What a sick human being. Brent thought someone like that should be thrown *beneath* the jail, not simply in a cell.

He laid one hand over hers. "Why didn't you tell me this last night?"

She looked at their hands a moment before raising her gaze back to his face. "I didn't want to involve you." She swallowed. "I didn't want you to get hurt too."

Zach came back in the room, followed by Michelle. "Stone said he'll be here in a few minutes."

"Shouldn't we meet him at Robin's house?" Brent asked.

"He's in the area. He'll talk to Robin here, then probably go over to her place." Zach sat on the coffee table once more. "Stone is a good guy, Robin. He'll do whatever he can to help you."

She nodded. She pulled her hands from beneath Brent's, crossed her arms over her breasts and rubbed her arms.

"Are you cold?" Brent asked.

"A little."

Michelle came back in the room, carrying a tray with three mugs of coffee. "I'll get you a sweater," she said after setting the tray on the coffee table.

"Thanks, Chelle." Brent picked up one of the mugs and handed it to Robin. "Here. This will help."

Robin took the mug from Brent and sipped the hot drink. She felt the warmth all the way down to her stomach. She hadn't been warm since the cold front blew into the area two days ago.

That wasn't true. She'd been warm wrapped in Brent's arms last night.

She stared into her coffee. He wanted to protect her from Stuart. She couldn't help wondering why. He'd become distant to her this morning after their shower. She'd interrupted him when he'd started to ask her a question, but surely that hadn't been enough for him to pull away from her the way he had. Not after the wonderful time they'd shared.

The front door buzzer rang, signaling someone had entered. Zach rose and left the room. He came back a moment later, followed by a tall, handsome man.

The man smiled at her and took Zach's place on the coffee table. "Ms. Howell, I'm Detective Evan Stone. Zach told me you're having some trouble with an old boyfriend."

With his long dark hair, neatly trimmed beard and powerful body, Evan Stone could be one of Coopers' Companions' escorts instead of a police detective. She looked into vivid green eyes that were filled with compassion and knew she could trust this man. She nodded.

Evan took a small notepad out of the back pocket of his jeans. "Why don't you start at the beginning and tell me everything?"

* * * * *

Robin pressed the button on the coffeemaker to start a second pot. The first one had disappeared quickly with five adults sharing it. Zach and Michelle had insisted on coming to her house with her, Brent and Evan. It was nice to have everyone around her, looking after her. That's something she'd never had in her life.

"The guys went outside," Michelle said, setting two empty mugs on the counter by Robin. "Zach and Brent insisted on going with Evan. At least they're smart enough to stay back and not step into something they shouldn't and mess up any possible evidence."

"Do you think there's evidence outside?"

Michelle shrugged. "Evan said Stuart had to get in your house some way. He's betting through a window."

"But all my windows are locked."

"We've known Evan for a long time. He's a great detective. If there's anything out there, he'll find it."

The subject of their conversation came in the back door, followed by Brent and Zach.

"Did you find anything?" Michelle asked.

"I know how he got in." Evan shrugged out of his jacket and draped it over the back of a kitchen chair. "He took the screen off your laundry room window. I found scratch marks on the bottom of the screen where he used a screwdriver or knife to wedge it off the window. This is an older house with old-fashioned windows and screens. A guy who knows what he's doing can get that screen off in seconds. Then he opens the window and crawls inside."

"But it's locked. All the windows are locked. And that window is higher off the ground than the others."

"Are you sure it's locked?"

Now that he'd put the doubt in her mind, Robin wasn't sure. "I opened it last week when the weather was so nice, but I'm sure I locked it again. At least, I thought I did."

"It's easy to forget something that's routine. How about if we check it now?"

Robin nodded. She led the way to the laundry room with Evan behind her. She'd feel incredibly stupid if she'd left an easy way for Stuart to get into her house.

Since the window was high in the wall, Robin couldn't see the lock. She had to reach up to feel it. The latch was closed.

"Stuart couldn't have gotten in this way."

"Let me take a look."

Robin moved back so Evan could step up to the window. He was a good six inches taller than she, so could see the latch. Taking a pair of latex gloves from his jeans pocket, he slipped them on his hands before examining the lock.

"Looks like it's loose."

"Where? I can't see."

Robin released a high squeak when strong hands clasped her waist and lifted her off the floor. A glance over her shoulder showed her Brent stood behind her.

Robin looked back at Evan to see his lips twitch. He quickly sobered. "Look here. The latch is broken. Stuart could've easily slipped a screwdriver beneath the latch so he could raise the window. You *did* lock it, but not really since it's broken."

"Well, I feel stupid."

"Don't. You didn't know the latch is broken." He tugged off his gloves and stuffed them back in his pocket. "You should call your landlord and tell him about it so he can get it repaired."

"I will." She looked over her shoulder at Brent. "You can let me down now."

She saw Evan's lips twitch again as Brent let her slide to the floor. "You said you received a note and box of candy from Stuart?"

"Yes. They're in my bedroom."

"I'll take them with me to check for prints. I dusted the window screen, but couldn't get a clear print from it. If he's as smart as you say he is, he probably wore gloves."

Robin's shoulders sagged. "Does that mean there's nothing you can do?"

"That means I may have to dig a little deeper." He gave her a cocky smile. "I don't give up easily."

Almost Perfection

The men followed her from the laundry room to her bedroom. After donning the latex gloves again, Evan slipped the note and box into a plastic zippered bag.

"I'd like you to come down to the station and have your prints taken. Then we can eliminate yours from any others we might find on these."

"Certainly. When should I do that?"

"Monday will be fine. Things don't exactly move at the speed of lightning in a police department."

Robin chuckled. She liked Evan. He'd made her feel at ease right away, even while telling him things about Stuart she'd rather forget.

"You told me Stuart was given a twenty-year sentence. Have you talked to anyone on the parole board or sheriff's department in Colorado about his early release?"

"No. I was going to call this morning, but..." She stopped and glanced at Brent. Waking up in Brent's arms had pushed Stuart totally out of her mind. "I forgot."

Evan also glanced at Brent. Robin wondered if somehow the detective knew Brent had spent the night with her.

"I have some contacts in Denver," Evan said. "Let me check first, see what I can find out for you."

"I'd appreciate that."

"One more thing. You should think about staying with someone. You shouldn't be alone."

She glanced at Brent. He leaned against her dresser, his ankles crossed, listening intently. "All the Coopers have offered me a place to stay."

"Good." Evan reached in his shirt pocket and drew out a business card. "Call me if you need anything."

"I will. Thank you."

"I'll find my way out." He slapped Brent on the shoulder as he passed him. "Take care of her."

"I plan to."

Robin wondered if she should be angry at Brent's "take charge" attitude. Strangely, she wasn't. She'd never had someone want to take care of her, protect her. It felt good to lean on someone for a change.

Brent moved away from the dresser and stepped closer to her. "Have you decided who you're going to stay with?"

It should be Michelle. They were almost the same age, seemed to have a lot in common and got along great. But Michelle already had a houseguest. Staying with her would be too much of an imposition.

Jade was a delight. Charming, friendly, generous. Robin knew Jade would welcome her for as long as Robin needed to stay. That's where she should go.

She opened her mouth to tell Brent her decision. Instead of saying what she'd intended, she said one word.

"You."

* * * * *

Brent glanced at Robin again. She hadn't said a word since she got in his car for the trip to his condo. She stared out her window, silent and still. He wished he knew what she was thinking.

Wanting to break the silence, he said the first thing that popped into his head. "I'm sorry your car isn't ready yet. Skip said he should have it ready first thing in the morning."

She didn't say anything, but continued to stare out the window.

"I'll take you anywhere you need to go. That isn't a problem."

"I know." She turned her head toward him and smiled weakly. "Thank you."

He didn't like this quiet, withdrawn Robin. He wanted the one with the fire, the one who wasn't afraid to pop back at him when he flew off the handle. "You know you can talk to me about anything, don't you?"

"I'm... Things are a bit overwhelming for me."

He could understand that. She'd been through a lot in one day. "Stone's the best. If anyone can find Holden, he will."

"But how? He could be anywhere in the Metroplex. Or anywhere in the state. He may have driven up from Houston or Austin or Waco to drop off his surprises, then went back."

"I doubt that. From the way you've described him, I'm sure he's close by so he can keep tabs on you."

Robin blew out a breath and laid her head back on the headrest. "I hate this! I thought I was through with Stuart when he went to prison. He has no right to come back into my life."

Brent reached over and took her hand. He would do everything he could to make sure she stayed safe. "We'll get him, Robin. I promise you that on my life."

Chapter Fourteen

I promise you that on my life.

Brent's words sent a chill down Robin's spine. He had no idea how true that could be. If she continued to stay involved with Brent, his life could be in danger.

She couldn't allow that to happen.

Brent pulled up to the gate of a luxurious condominium complex. The gate opened after he punched in a code on the entrance keypad. Robin admired the beautiful landscaping as Brent drove toward the back of the complex.

"This was Zach's condo," he said, pulling into a covered parking space. "I bought it from him when he and Jade moved into their house." He looked at her and grinned. "I got a hell of a deal."

He climbed out of the car and opened the back door to get Robin's suitcase. She had no idea how long she'd stay here, so hadn't been sure what to pack. She'd ended up with two changes of clothes. She hoped she wouldn't have to impose on Brent any longer than two days.

He unlocked the front door and pushed it open for Robin. She stepped past the entryway and into a sunken living room decorated in neutral, rust and dark green. A quick glance around the room at the masculine surroundings and it was obvious a man lived here alone.

"Michelle bugs me about adding what she calls feminine touches. I told her I'm not feminine, so I don't need that kind of stuff."

"Some knickknacks on those bookshelves would be nice."

"Just more to dust."

"Sorry. I'll never believe you do the dusting. I'll bet you have a housekeeper come in once a week."

"Twice," Brent said with a grin.

Robin laughed at his confession. At least he was honest.

"Your room is this way."

He picked up her suitcase that he'd set inside the front door and led the way down the short hall. Robin couldn't help but notice he'd said "your room", not "my room". Opening a door on the right, he motioned for Robin to enter before him. The bedroom carried the same color scheme as the living room.

Brent set her suitcase on the bed. "How about if I go get us something to eat while you unpack and do whatever you need to do?"

She didn't know how she'd put anything in her churning stomach, but she nodded.

"Do you like Chinese? There's a great restaurant about three blocks from here."

"Sure. That sounds good."

"I'll get us a variety. Do you have a favorite dish?"

"Broccoli and beef."

Brent smiled. "You got it. Be back in about half an hour."

She waited until she heard the front door close before venturing out of the bedroom. Turning right, she walked through an open door into Brent's bedroom. Much larger than the guest room, it reflected the same masculine furnishings that she'd seen so far. The stark, abstract paintings on the walls wouldn't give anyone a hint of Brent's personality. Perhaps that's the way he wanted it. Perhaps he didn't want anyone to know he had a kind heart underneath that shallow exterior.

He'd proven to her that he wasn't simply an arrogant ass by inviting her into his home...a place that was his private sanctuary. She hadn't believed him at first when he said he never brought women here. Michelle had confirmed it this afternoon. Brent dated a lot of women, but he came home alone.

She wandered into his bath, noting the wide, oval bathtub and glass shower stall. Both of them were large enough to easily hold two people. She pictured Brent and her sipping wine in the tub, surrounded by bubbles and candlelight.

Her fantasy probably wouldn't come true. If Brent wanted to be with her, he would've taken her suitcase into his bedroom, not the guest room.

She couldn't help the disappointment, even though she'd known all along her time with Brent would be brief. He wasn't looking for happily ever after. Robin doubted if the word "permanent" was even in his vocabulary.

Knowing that any kind of future with Brent would be impossible, Robin decided to enjoy what time she had with him. She wouldn't cling or cry. She accepted that some couples simply weren't meant to be together.

Her next stop was the kitchen. She peeked inside the refrigerator, but quickly closed it when she heard the front door open. Brent had gotten back quicker than she'd expected.

"Robin?"

"In the kitchen."

He stepped into the room, carrying a large paper sack. "What are you doing?"

She shrugged. "Snooping."

Brent chuckled. "Find anything interesting?"

"Not in here. I haven't gone through your bathroom cabinets yet."

"The most exciting thing you'll find in *my* bathroom cabinets is an outdated bottle of aspirin."

"How boring."

He set his bag on the countertop. "Would you like to sit at the dining room table, or have a picnic on the living room floor?"

"I vote for a picnic."

"If you'll grab a couple of plates and forks, I'll open this." He removed a bottle of cold Chardonnay from the bag. "Luckily, there's a liquor store close to the restaurant."

"How convenient."

She found the plates and silverware, and also grabbed several large spoons for serving. "Napkins?"

"Dining room buffet. Michelle made sure I have plenty of cloth napkins. I'm happy with paper towels."

By the time Robin stepped into the living room, Brent was on his knees, setting out the little white containers on the coffee table in front of the sectional sofa. She dropped to the floor beside him, sinking into the deep carpeting. "Do you think you bought enough food?"

"I like leftovers." He took a box out of the bag and set it directly in front of her. "Broccoli and beef."

"It smells wonderful."

"I suppose you're going to eat all that by yourself."

She grinned. "Maybe."

Brent returned her grin before joining her on the floor. "I think I can survive on the other six dishes I got." He poured the wine into two glasses and handed one to her. "Cheers."

"Cheers."

The wine slid smoothly down her throat. She took another sip before opening the container of broccoli and beef and spooning some onto her plate. When she'd taken what she wanted, she passed the box to Brent.

"Oh, so you *are* going to share."

His eyes twinkled with amusement. She truly enjoyed this side of Brent, the one who liked to tease. "That's only fair, since you bought everything."

"It's never a hardship for me to eat Chinese."

Robin chose a spoonful from each container. She ate silently, enjoying the delicious food and the company of the man sitting beside her.

"How do you feel?" Brent asked softly.

She could lie and say fine, but she wouldn't lie to Brent. "I'm having a hard time believing all this is real. Stuart should be behind bars, not free to terrorize me."

"Is it possible he's still in prison and arranged for someone to break into your house and leave that message on your computer and the candy?"

Robin hadn't considered Stuart could somehow convince someone to do his dirty work. "I suppose it's possible, but I don't think it's probable. Why wait seven years? If he'd wanted to hurt me, he could've started the scare campaign a long time ago."

"If he's as demented as he sounds, he might've wanted to lull you into a...sense of security before he contacted you."

The churning in her stomach returned. Robin laid her fork on her half-empty plate. "I don't understand why he wouldn't accept my breaking up with him. Couples break up all the time when things don't work out. I'm no one special that he should've tried so hard to keep me."

"I disagree with that. I think you're very special."

He quickly picked up his wineglass and took a healthy sip. Robin wondered if he was sorry he'd paid her the compliment.

Brent set down his glass and picked up his fork again. "He must've had good qualities or you wouldn't have fallen in love with him."

"He had wonderful qualities, at first. He was kind, attentive, charming, generous, handsome. Every woman's dream man."

"When did he change?"

"A little over a year after we started going together. He demanded more and more of my time. He complained when I wanted to go to a movie or shopping with girlfriends. The more he complained, the more I wanted to get away. I felt like he was smothering me." She dipped a fried wonton in the sweet and sour sauce on her plate. "I believe in a couple being together, but they also need time alone or with other friends."

"I believe that too. I know Jade and her daughter go shopping almost every Saturday. They've done it for years. Zach would never complain about Jade spending time with Breanna."

He picked up the bottle of wine and splashed some into her glass. "You've mentioned several times about taking care of yourself your whole life. What happened to your parents?"

Robin rarely talked about her parents. Although she'd lost them years ago, there were times when the pain was so fresh. "My father left us when I was eight. I don't know why. My mother never told me why he left. She was devastated. She barely ate or slept for almost two years. She stopped caring for herself or for me. I had to..."

She stopped. She doubted if Brent truly wanted to know everything she went through as a child. "She finally swallowed a bottle of sleeping pills."

"How old were you?"

"Ten."

"Jesus," he breathed.

Her throat tightened at the memory of finding her mother's body in her bed. She pushed the mental picture aside and sipped her wine.

"Did you go live with grandparents, or an aunt and uncle?"

Robin shook her head. "I didn't have any family. I went into the foster care system. Some homes were good, some not so good. But I did what I had to do. I finished school with good grades and went to college mostly on scholarships. I waitressed for spending money."

She decided this conversation had turned much too serious. It was time to inject some humor. She grinned. "I learned to carry three plates on one arm."

"Now there's a talent everyone should have."

Picking up her wineglass, she held it with both hands. "I was so young when I met Stuart. He completely swept me off my feet. I fell hard and fast. That's probably why I didn't see his true nature until I was in over my head." She chuckled without humor. "Pretty pathetic, huh?"

"No." His gaze touched every part of her face. "Not pathetic at all."

He looked at her so intently, she wondered if he would kiss her. She licked her bottom lip in anticipation.

Instead of the kiss she desired, Brent picked up two wrapped fortune cookies. "Ready for dessert?"

A fortune cookie wasn't the kind of dessert she had in mind. "Sure."

Tearing off the plastic wrapper, Robin broke the cookie in half. She tugged the small piece of paper from the treat and unfolded it.

"*Love will find you when you least expect it.* Well, that's certainly a generic fortune."

"They usually are." Brent cracked open his own cookie and pulled out the piece of paper. Robin waited for him to read his fortune aloud. He remained silent.

"What does it say?"

He handed the paper to her. Robin gasped softly when she read the exact same words that had been on her fortune.

"What do you think the odds are of us getting the same fortune?" Brent asked.

"Probably higher than winning the lottery."

"Yeah." He tipped up his wineglass and drained it in one swallow. "Did you get enough to eat?"

"I ate enough for the next three days."

"There's plenty for a midnight snack if you get hungry later." He reached behind him, picked up a remote from the sofa cushion and handed it to her. "Why don't you find a movie or something for us to watch while I clean up?"

"I'll help you."

She rose to her knees, but Brent touched her shoulder to stop her. "No, you stay here and get comfortable. I won't be long."

He poured the rest of the wine into their glasses, then placed the containers in the paper sack and gathered up their dirty dishes and silverware. "I have DVDs too, if you can't find anything on TV. Michelle bought several of them, so I'm sure you'll find a lot of chick flicks. They're in the cabinet beneath the TV."

Curious to what he considered "chick flicks", Robin knelt in front of the cabinet and perused the titles. He had dozens, ranging from war movies to westerns to romances. She'd bet Michelle bought the romances.

She selected one and rose as Brent came back in the room. "Did you find one you like?"

She held the case up so he could see it. He nodded. "That'll work. It isn't *too* sappy."

"Sappy is good for you."

Robin settled on the sofa with her feet curled beside her hip and a throw pillow over her lap. Brent sat beside her, only a few inches away. He handed her wineglass to her, picked up his own and pointed the remote toward the television.

* * * * *

Brent slipped his hands beneath his head and stared at the ceiling. Eleven o'clock and he wasn't the least bit sleepy.

He'd asked Robin if she wanted to watch another movie after the first one was over. She'd said she was tired and went to her room, leaving him alone to go to his own room.

Now he lay here in the dark, alone, with thoughts of touching Robin running through his mind.

He hadn't wanted her to think he expected her to have sex with him just because he'd invited her to stay with him. That's why he'd put her suitcase in the guest room, even though he'd wanted to bring it in here. He thought about reaching for her in the middle of the night, drawing her body against his. Her ass fit perfectly against his cock.

Brent groaned as that part of his anatomy responded. Being close to Robin had made him half hard all evening. It had taken more willpower than he thought he possessed not to touch her, kiss her.

Plus, there'd been those damn fortune cookies.

Turning on the lamp, Brent sat up and stuffed two pillows behind his back. He picked up the small piece of paper from the nightstand. He and Robin had found the same fortune in their cookies. He'd blame Michelle or Zach for the coincidence if he hadn't known they didn't have anything to do with this.

Love will find you when you least expect it.

He had no idea why he'd kept this little piece of paper. It meant nothing. There were probably hundreds of people eating Chinese tonight who'd received the same fortune. Just because he and Robin had both gotten it didn't mean they were supposed to be together.

But he wanted to be with her. He wanted to make love to her and then fall asleep with her in his arms.

Brent threw back the covers, climbed out of bed and crossed to his dresser. Opening the second drawer, he grabbed the pair of sweat pants on top. Not bothering with any kind of shirt, he left his bedroom.

Light shone beneath Robin's door, so she must not be asleep. He stepped up to her door and knocked softly.

"Come in."

He turned the knob and opened the door. Robin sat in the middle of the bed, pillows behind her back and a book on her lap. The covers were bunched around her waist. She wore a silky gold top or nightgown edged with ivory lace that flowed over her breasts.

"Can't you sleep?" he asked.

She shook her head. "I thought reading a while would make me sleepy."

Her gaze traveled over his body as he approached the bed. The sweat pants wouldn't do a very good job of hiding his partial hard-on from her. She continued to watch him as he sat on the edge of the bed. "I'm not sleepy either." He took the book from her hands and set it on the nightstand. With one finger, he tipped up her chin and lowered his lips to hers.

He heard her sharp intake of breath, then the low moan in her throat. He kissed her gently, tenderly, his lips moving over hers so slowly. He sipped at her lips, tickled the corners of her mouth with his tongue.

"Brent," she whispered.

He nipped the delicate skin beneath her chin. "Come to bed with me."

She cradled his face in her hands and kissed him. "Yes."

Chapter Fifteen

Brent drew back the covers so Robin could rise. He received an enticing view of her thighs before she stood and her nightgown fell to her knees. Taking her hand, he led her to his bedroom.

He closed the door behind them and faced Robin. Right now, he wished he'd taken Michelle's advice. He wanted to make love with Robin with her body bathed in candlelight.

"I should have candles."

"I don't need candles." She slid her hands across his chest and over his shoulders. "I only need you."

Her arms encircled his neck as she rose to her tiptoes and kissed him. Her lips moved over his, her tongue swept into his mouth. Brent wrapped his arms around her and pulled her body close to his. He shifted his hips from side to side, brushing his cock against her mound.

She moaned.

He loved that sound. He gripped her buttocks and pulled her closer to his rod. Her ass was round and firm and filled his palms perfectly. He could hear the *swish swish* of the silky material as the gown glided over her skin. He gripped her ass tighter while dropping kisses down her throat.

He could spend a lifetime tasting her skin and never tire of it.

"Brent."

The barest of whispers made him lift his head and look into her eyes. They appeared luminous in the soft lamplight. "What do you need me to do?"

"Touch me. Everywhere."

Obeying that order wouldn't be a problem at all. He gathered the hem of her gown and pulled it up her body. Robin raised her arms. Brent tugged the gown over her head and dropped it on the floor.

She wore nothing beneath it.

He studied her body...the full breasts with dark pink nipples, the flat stomach, the flared hips, the blonde curls on her mound. His gaze swept all the way to her feet before journeying back up her body. The sight of her caused his throat to tighten and his heart to pound.

"God, Robin, you're so lovely."

She smiled tenderly. "Thank you." She pointedly looked at his groin. "I'd like to see you too."

Brent chuckled. "Is that a polite way of telling me to strip?"

"Stripping would be good."

Seconds later, he stood nude before her. He kicked his sweats aside and drew her back into his arms. "Better?"

"Much."

She wrapped her arms around his neck again and kissed him. Brent buried his hands in her hair and tilted her head so he could deepen the kiss. Lips slid across lips, tongues stroked, breaths mingled. His body touched hers from chest to thighs. Her skin felt so soft, so smooth beneath his hands.

He jerked when her fingers wrapped around his cock, then groaned as she began a milking motion. "Careful. You don't want this over before we even get started."

Her fingers drifted down his body. "I'm not worried. I know how quickly you recuperate."

Brent widened his stance to give her more room to touch him. She cuddled close, nuzzling and nipping at his neck. Her other hand traveled up and down his back while she palmed his balls and gave them a gentle massage. They drew up tighter to his body the longer she touched them. He'd never come from a woman playing with his balls. Tonight might be a first.

Despite the pleasure of her touch, Brent pulled her hand away from him. Her satisfaction had to come before his. He moved backward until he could climb on the bed, tugging Robin with him until they were on their knees in the middle. Brent drew her into his arms for more kisses. He couldn't get enough of her mouth, her taste.

He longed to taste every part of her body.

Robin's fingers wrapped around his cock again. He inhaled sharply when he felt the fingernails of her other hand dig into one buttock.

"Witch," he growled.

She gave him a devilish smile. "I couldn't resist."

"You do realize you'll have to pay for that."

"How?"

Brent lifted her against him and laid her on the bed. He covered her body with his as he kissed her again. Cradling one breast, he thumbed her nipple over and over. Each pass of his thumb made Robin moan.

She reached between their bodies and clasped his shaft again. "Inside me, Brent. Please."

Once more, he pulled her fingers away from him. Taking both her wrists in his hands, he held them over her head. "You're much too impatient."

A frown turned down her lips. "Since when doesn't a man want a woman who's horny?"

"Since he wants to savor her."

"Oh." Robin's lips curved into a smile. "Savoring is nice."

He chuckled. He'd never been with a woman who made him laugh during sex. Everything was different with Robin.

He didn't know *why* everything was different, but he planned to enjoy it.

She arched her back, pressing her breasts against his chest. "Are you going to hold my arms all night or do something?"

He liked playing with her. "I'll make a deal with you."

"What kind of deal?"

"I'll let go of your arms if you'll leave them where they are."

Her eyes narrowed. "Why?"

"I have some ideas." He placed his mouth near her ear and whispered, "Leave them there and I'll lick your clit 'til you come."

Heat filled her eyes. Her tongue passed over her lower lip. "Okay."

Brent kissed her, long and slow and deep. His hand rested between her breasts. He could feel her rapid heartbeat, the rise and fall of her chest with every breath. He kissed her lips once more before beginning the slow journey down her body. His tongue whisked across her collarbone and over the tops of her breasts. Each nipple received a leisurely lick, then a gentle suckling.

Robin arched her back again, but left her hands where he'd placed them. He rewarded her obedience by sucking harder on her nipples. He watched Robin's face as he flicked the hard tips with his tongue. Her lips were parted, her breath coming in pants. Her eyes were closed, her hands clenched into fists.

He pinched one nipple. She gasped. He thought at first he may have hurt her, until she moaned.

"Do you like this?" Drawing the peak into his mouth again, he ran his tongue around the areola.

She answered his question with another moan.

"Maybe I should suck your nipples until you come."

"Yes, please." Her voice was little more than a rasp.

Brent rose to his knees between hers, using his legs to push Robin's wide apart. She placed her feet on the bed and let her knees fall open. He swallowed hard at the sight of her clit peeking out from the hood. A drop of her cream ran down between the cheeks of her ass.

"Oh yeah. Your pussy is nice and wet."

Cradling her breasts in his hands, he kneaded both mounds as his mouth moved from one tip to the other. He bit the turgid peaks, soothed the bites with his tongue.

"Brent." Her voice sounded breathless and husky. "More. Please."

All too happy to follow orders, Brent pulled her nipple deep into his mouth and sucked hard. Robin clutched the pillow and writhed beneath him. He continued to suckle while squeezing and tugging on her other peak.

"Brent! *Ohhhhhhhh.*"

She grabbed his head, her body trembling. He kept kneading her breasts and licking her nipples, wanting to prolong her pleasure as long as possible.

Her hold loosened on his head and she ran her fingers through his hair. "That was... Wow."

One more gentle suck on each tip and he raised his head. "Feel good?"

Robin nodded. "I've never done that."

"You've never come from a man sucking your nipples?"

"No."

He'd given her something no man had ever given her. Fresh desire surged into his cock. He wondered what other ways he could make her come.

Rising to his knees once again, he slid his hand down her stomach and fingered her clit. "I hope you don't think you're through."

Her eyes rolled back when he began to caress her. "No, I don't think I'm through."

"Arms over your head."

She obeyed him instantly. Her eagerness proved to him that she wanted more.

His fingertips glided over her swollen flesh. More of her cream dribbled between her buttocks and pooled around her anus. He wanted to taste her more than he wanted to breathe.

"Turn over."

He helped her roll to her stomach, a pillow beneath her hips. Spreading her buttocks with his thumbs, he stared at her wet pussy. He dragged his thumb up through her feminine lips, gathering the moisture to smooth over her anus.

A sound came from Robin, a cross between a moan and a gasp. "Do you want me to stop?"

"No."

He spread more cream over her anus in a circular motion. Robin lifted her hips, as if silently asking for more.

Brent caressed her flesh a moment before pushing his thumb inside her ass. "Nice and tight. I like that." Leaning over her body, he nipped her earlobe. "I believe I said something about licking your clit." He pushed his thumb farther inside her. "How about if I start here?"

Robin rose to her elbows and looked at him over her shoulder. "You ask way too many unnecessary questions."

He shared a kiss with her, then returned to his spot between her legs. Lying on his stomach, he spread her buttocks again. One swipe of his tongue from her clit to her anus and he groaned. She tasted better than the most succulent food, the richest drink, the most decadent dessert. He licked the full length of her labia again.

"That feels so good," she said, her voice breathless.

"You taste incredible." He drove his tongue into her channel, licked her entire length again. He'd always loved oral sex, and especially enjoyed it with Robin. "Delicious."

The breathy little noises in her throat urged him to move his tongue faster over her intimate flesh. He concentrated on her clit for several moments before moving to her anus. She inhaled sharply and lifted her hips higher.

Pulling her buttocks farther apart, he drove his tongue into her ass. Robin jerked and moaned loudly. Brent laved the sensitive area over and over with the flat of his tongue, then fucked her ass with the tip.

Robin's movements became more frantic, her breathing quicker. He held her buttocks tightly, holding her in place while he thrust his tongue inside her ass again and again. She froze for a moment, then released a keening moan and trembled.

Brent pulled back and watched her anus contract while the waves of her orgasm washed over her. Once her body stilled again, he leaned over her back, his rigid cock nestled between her buttocks. He dropped soft kisses on her shoulder.

"I love it when you come."

Laughing, she pushed her hair back from her face. "I love it when I do too." She reached back and ran her fingers over his cheek. "What about you?"

"I'm not in a hurry." He opened the nightstand drawer and withdrew a small bottle of lubricant and a condom. "Okay if I play a little?"

She nodded.

Flipping open the top, Brent drizzled a stream of lube on her anus. Robin gasped and clenched her buttocks.

"That's cold!"

"It'll warm up soon." He waited until she relaxed to touch her again. He spread the lube generously before pushing his thumb inside her again. "Damn, you've got a great ass."

Quickly donning the condom, Brent slipped his cock inside her pussy. He closed his eyes and sighed. Her channel was so tight, so creamy. He began to thrust slow and steady, matching his movements to the lifting of her hips. He could smell her musky arousal with every movement.

Brent applied lube to his fingers and pushed one past her anus. He continued to thrust as he added a second finger with the first. She buried her face in her pillow and whimpered. That sound of pleasure spurred him to move faster.

"You like having me in your pussy and ass at the same time?"

"Yessssssss."

He shoved his fingers all the way inside her. "How about if I fuck you here?"

Robin threw back her head. "Yesssssss."

Blood surging faster, heart thumping, Brent withdrew his cock from Robin's pussy and thrust into her ass. She didn't tighten or gasp in pain, but arched her hips higher to take him deeper.

"God, you are so hot." He pumped into her with short, quick jabs, then long, slow thrusts. "*Fuck*, this feels good."

She reached back and dug her fingernails into one of his buttocks. "Brent! Yes. Yes, yes, *yes*!"

The clamping of her muscles around his cock signaled her orgasm, and pushed him over the edge into his own.

His strength deserted him and he fell on top of her. A soft "oomph" from Robin's lips made Brent prop himself on his elbows to take some of his weight off her. He lay still, dropping gentle kisses on her shoulder and upper back. He brushed his fingers across a wrinkled scar on her left shoulder blade before giving it a long kiss.

Tenderness welled up inside him, even stronger than this morning. He couldn't imagine why any man would want to hurt a woman as wonderful as Robin.

"I'll be right back," he whispered.

He reluctantly withdrew from her body and went into the bathroom. If anyone could find Holden, it would be Stone. He found clues where no one else did. In the meantime, Brent would protect Robin and make sure Holden never got near her.

Whatever it took to stop the bastard, he'd do it.

Brent opened the bathroom door. Robin's gaze traveled down his body as he walked to the bed. His cock stirred when he saw her look directly at his groin.

He ignored that stirring and turned off the lamp. Crawling into bed next to her, he drew her into his arms, her back to his chest. "You okay?" he asked after kissing her shoulder.

"I'm wonderful. I've never had so many orgasms in so short a time."

He chuckled, low and throaty. "Happy to be of service, ma'am."

Brent caressed her stomach with one hand, cradled her breast with the other. She felt good in his arms, in his bed. Sighing softly, he closed his eyes and waited for sleep to take him.

"Why did you pull away from me this morning?" Robin asked.

He opened his eyes again. The question didn't surprise him. He wondered why she hadn't asked it sooner. He thought about how to answer it, and decided to be totally honest. "I was scared."

"By?"

"The way you make me feel."

"How do I make you feel?" she asked in a bare whisper.

He thumbed her nipple until it turned into a hard peak. Sex he understood. Sex he could handle. Feelings were completely different. "This is all brand new territory for me, Robin. I enjoy being with you. The sex is the best I've ever had. I want to protect you. But..." He stopped.

"But what?" she asked after he remained silent several moments.

"I don't know where this is going."

Robin rolled to her side to face him. "It doesn't have to go anywhere, Brent. I'm not asking for anything from you." She cupped his cheek, caressed his lips with her thumb. "I knew the first time we made love that you aren't looking for anything permanent. I accept that."

He should be grateful she had no intention of pushing for something he didn't want. Instead, he wasn't sure if he liked her easy acceptance of a sex-only relationship.

"Did I say something wrong?" Robin asked.

"No, not at all."

To prove his words, he kissed her. She returned his kiss, her lips soft and yielding. His cock stirred again, ready to love her once more. He slid his hand down her stomach to between her thighs. Her pussy was still slick with her juices and the lube.

The lure of that silky flesh was too much to resist.

Brent quickly donned a condom and eased between Robin's spread legs. He kissed her again as he drove his shaft into her wet heat. She moved with him, meeting every thrust until she trembled with her climax. Only then did he allow his own orgasm to peak.

Exhausted, satisfied, he moved to his side and tugged Robin close to him. After one final kiss on her lips, he closed his eyes.

Chapter Sixteen

Stuart touched the knife blade with his thumb. He smiled. Nice and sharp and ready to use.

He didn't look forward to hurting Brent. He'd thought the tire thing would make Robin tell Brent to take a hike. She had to have known that was a sign from him. After the notes and candy he'd left her, she knew he was close and watching her every move.

Instead, she was in Brent's condo—and probably in his bed—right now.

Stuart winced when the knife nicked his thumb. He watched a bead of dark red blood well up from the small cut. How fascinating.

It would be even more fascinating to watch Brent's blood bubble up from several cuts.

He wasn't sure when. It had to be the perfect time, the perfect place. Stuart had no intention of going back to prison. Brent's demise wouldn't be linked to him. Robin would know, yet no one would be able to prove he had anything to do with Brent's death.

Once Brent was out of the way, he'd get Robin back. They'd be together forever, just the way he'd planned from the moment he met her.

She belonged to him. He'd make sure she never forgot that.

* * * * *

Robin squirmed at the feel of a wet tongue across her nipple. Sighing softly, she arched her back to get closer to that warm caress. "Mmmmmm."

The sound of a wicked chuckle made her open her eyes. Brent's eyes twinkled with humor as he tickled her nipple with the end of his tongue.

"Good morning," he said before licking the hard tip again.

"Good morning."

"I really enjoyed our early morning sex yesterday." He slid his hand over her stomach and to between her thighs. "How about a repeat?"

Robin flinched when he touched sensitive flesh. She wasn't used to all the lovemaking she'd had the last two days.

"Sore?" he asked.

"A little tender."

"Too tender to come on my tongue?"

Her pussy clenched at the thought. She doubted if she'd ever be too tender for that. But she didn't want to be selfish and take pleasure from Brent without returning it. "That works both ways, you know."

Heat flashed in his eyes. "Does it?"

Robin nodded. She ran her hand through his tousled hair. "I'd like to taste you."

"I think we'd better shower first." He rose to his knees. The covers fell away from him, exposing his hard cock to her. She could change her mind. Surely it wouldn't hurt that much to have him inside her again.

He flashed her a crooked grin. "You're staring at the merchandise."

"I like to shop."

Brent chuckled. "I offered. You refused."

"Can I change my mind?"

Taking her hands, he pulled her into a sitting position. "After our shower."

"Or during our shower, like yesterday."

The humor faded from his expression. Looking down at their joined hands, he rubbed his thumbs over her skin. "I need to talk to you about that."

She didn't know what she'd said to make him turn so serious. "Okay."

"I didn't wear a condom." He looked back into her eyes. "You said you haven't been with a man in a long time. I have regular checkups and I'm very careful, so I'm not worried about diseases. But what about birth control? Do you use anything?"

"I'm protected. You don't have to worry about that."

She saw the apology in his eyes before he kissed her. "I'm sorry. I never should have put you in the position of having to ask you. I saw your body through the shower curtain and I…" He blew out a breath. "It's not an excuse, I know, but I didn't think about anything but touching you."

"Should I be flattered that I made you lose your head?"

It pleased her to see the humor return to his eyes. "You definitely did that."

He released her hands and cradled her face. His lips touched hers as the phone rang.

"Lousy timing." He gave her one more quick kiss. "Hold that pucker."

Robin burrowed beneath the covers while Brent looked at the phone's display. "It's Michelle." He slid underneath the covers with her and picked up the receiver. "Hey, sis…When?…Yeah, we'll be there…What?" He chuckled and shook his head. "Okay, I'll do it…I won't forget the pecan ones…And your latte…Bye."

Brent pressed the off button on the phone. "Stone called Zach a few minutes ago. He has some news for us. He'll be at

Coopers' Companions in about an hour. Chelle and Zach will meet us there."

"You said something about pecan ones and latte."

"There's a bakery a few blocks from here that makes incredible pastries. Chelle put in an order for the pecan Danish and a latte."

"Make that two."

Brent laughed. "You got it."

* * * * *

"I spoke with Lieutenant Briggins of the Denver County sheriff's department," Evan said, flipping open his small notepad. "Stuart Holden was released on parole five months ago. In Colorado, victims are notified of parole hearings and when someone is released. Briggins said they attempted to contact you, but you'd moved."

"I left Colorado right after Stuart's trial. I know he was given twenty years in prison."

"He got twenty years, but his sentence was pleaded down from first degree arson to a crime of passion. That made him eligible for parole in seven years." He turned a page on his notepad. "Holden was a model prisoner. He kept to himself, didn't cause any problems, no fights. I'm not surprised he made parole the first time he went before the board." More pages rustled as he read over his notes. "Robin, you said you found the note and candy from Holden on Thursday."

"Yes, after I got home from Jade and Zach's house."

"Nothing from him before that?"

Robin shook her head. "No."

"And Monday was the first day you came here to Coopers' Companions?"

She didn't understand what that had to do with anything, but answered honestly. "Yes."

A frown crossed Evan's face while he studied his notes. "What are you thinking, Stone?" Zach asked.

"I'm wondering why he waited five months to contact Robin."

"He didn't know where she was," Brent said.

"Maybe. Maybe not. It's too much of a coincidence to me that he's been out of prison for five months, yet didn't contact Robin until she took a job here." Evan rubbed one finger across his mustache. "It's almost as if…" He stopped.

"As if what?" Robin asked.

Evan looked from Zach to Brent to Michelle and back to Zach. "Could Holden be one of your escorts? He's probably using another identity."

"No way," Brent said firmly. "We thoroughly check out all our guys."

"Is there one who's been with you five months or less?"

"Three," Zach said. "Jim Bradshaw and Clarke Woodall started four months ago, Rubin Hall two months ago. Robin's met Clarke. He was at the photo shoot Tuesday night."

"We haven't heard from Jim or Rubin this week," Brent said. "I sent out an email to all the escorts about taking pictures for Coopers' Companions' new website. Neither of them answered it. No phone calls either."

"I can't believe either of them could be involved in this," Michelle said. "They're both great guys."

"I'm sure Holden was too, at one time." Evan jotted down their names on his notepad. "Am I right, Robin?"

She nodded.

"I ran a check on Holden. No job, no credit cards, no bank accounts, at least not in his real name. He disappeared after he left prison."

"He broke his parole," Zach said.

Evan nodded. "Big time."

"So he could be anywhere." Suddenly chilled, Robin crossed her arms over her stomach. "There's no way to catch him."

"I told you I don't give up easily." Evan faced Zach again. "Holden has olive skin, dark brown hair and brown eyes. His hair was shoulder-length and he had a mustache when he was arrested, but could've easily cut both to change his appearance. Briggins promised to email me Holden's picture. Their network was down when I spoke to him and he couldn't do it then."

"Both Jim and Rubin match that description." Zach looked at his sister. "Don't we have their pictures in our files?"

Michelle nodded. "I'll get them."

Robin watched Michelle rise from the dining room table and leave the room. The Danish and latte she'd had earlier churned in her stomach. To think Stuart could've been here, right in this chair where she sat now.

She looked at Brent sitting next to her. "Did you tell Evan about your tires?"

"No. Why should I?"

"What about your tires?" Evan asked.

Robin turned back to the detective. "Brent had all the tires slashed on his SUV while he was at my house. He thinks some kids did it, but I think it was Stuart. It was a message for Brent to stay away from me."

"That's not gonna happen." Brent took her hand, interlacing their fingers. "He isn't going to scare me away from you, no matter what."

Michelle came back in the room, carrying two file folders. She placed them on the table in front of Robin and took the chair next to her. Robin opened the one with Rubin's name on it. She studied the picture in the plastic pocket on the left side of the folder. A handsome, dark-haired man with a charming smile stared back at her. Her heart slowed its frantic beat when she realized she didn't know him.

"This isn't Stuart."

"Are you sure?" Evan asked. "People can change a lot in seven years."

"I'm sure." She opened the other folder. She saw a picture of an even more handsome man in the plastic sleeve. "This isn't Stuart either."

"Do you have a picture of him, Robin?"

Robin shook her head. "Not anymore. I threw everything away that had anything to do with him."

"I hate to ask you to do this, but maybe you should look at pictures of all the escorts, just to be sure none of them are Holden."

"Come to my office with me," Michelle said to Robin. "All the files are there."

Brent waited until the women left the room before turning to Evan. "Now what?"

"I keep looking. My gut tells me Holden coming after Robin now is somehow connected to your business. If he isn't one of your escorts, then he's a friend of one."

Brent's stomach tightened at the thought that one of their escorts could be the cause of Robin's dilemma. "How can we help?"

"You're doing it by staying close to Robin. She shouldn't be alone."

"She won't be. I'll handcuff her to me if necessary."

Evan grinned. "That could be fun."

Michelle led Robin back into the room a few minutes later. "Anything?" Brent asked as Robin returned to her chair next to him.

She shook her head. "Stuart isn't one of your escorts."

"Thank God," Zach said.

"It'd be better if he *was* one of our escorts," Brent said. "Then he'd be easier to find. Hell, we know dozens of guys with brown hair and eyes."

"He thinks he's above the law," Evan said, "so he's arrogant and doesn't believe he'll get caught. He'll make a mistake. That's when we'll get him."

* * * * *

Robin lay still with her eyes closed, not wanting to move and possibly wake Brent. She was warm and comfortable in his arms and didn't want this time to end.

He'd been so generous with her, so caring. After Evan left Coopers' Companions yesterday morning, she and Michelle had decided to work on the website. Brent and Zach had picked up lunch for them, and her car from the repair shop. She felt better having her own car back, even though Brent had declared she wouldn't be driving anywhere by herself.

She wondered if she should be more upset by his command. Instead, she appreciated his desire to protect her.

Shifting to a different position, her buttocks brushed against Brent's hard cock. She could turn over and wake him with a kiss. Better yet, she could wake him by taking him in her mouth. She hadn't had the chance to taste him.

Making love with Brent was amazing, yet she didn't want that this morning. She wanted to stay close to him, wrapped in his arms, more than she wanted sex.

He stirred behind her and dropped a kiss on her shoulder. "Are you awake?" he asked, his voice raspy.

"I am."

"For how long?"

"A few minutes."

"Why didn't you wake me?"

"Because I'm comfortable and don't want to move."

His arm tightened around her waist. He kissed her shoulder again. "I like waking up next to you."

"I like it too."

He remained silent for several seconds. "I guess you feel that against your butt."

Robin smiled to herself. "I do."

"Any ideas what to do with it?"

"Ignore it?"

"That wasn't exactly the response I'd hoped to get from you."

She giggled, then rolled over to face him. "I'll tell you what I *do* want."

"What?"

She laid one arm across his chest and propped her chin on it. "I want one of your Western omelets. Maybe with some hash browns or fried potatoes."

"I have a raging hard-on and you're thinking of *omelets*?"

She giggled again at the disappointed look in his eyes. "And biscuits with strawberry preserves."

He released an exaggerated sigh. "The sacrifices men make for their women."

The humor in his eyes showed her he wasn't upset, but enjoyed their playful banter. She kissed the center of his chest. "I'll help cook."

The music of *The Good, The Bad and The Ugly* coming from Brent's cell phone stopped him before he made another comment about cooking versus sex. He liked the idea of preparing breakfast with Robin in his kitchen. He'd never done that with a woman.

There were many things he'd never done in his life that he was now experiencing with Robin. So far, he'd enjoyed every one of them.

He picked up the phone from the nightstand and flipped it open. "Mornin', Zach."

"Mornin'. You busy?"

"Not yet. I'm trying to convince Robin that sex would be better than cooking breakfast."

Zach laughed. "Any luck?"

"Not so far."

"I'm glad I didn't interrupt anything 'cause I need your help. Mom called me a few minutes ago. She doesn't have any hot water."

"Probably the heating element."

"That's what I think too. How about riding over there with me? It's probably just the element, but she may need a new hot water heater."

Normally, Brent wouldn't hesitate to help his mother, but he didn't want to leave Robin alone. "What about Robin?"

"What about me?"

"Just a sec, Zach." He moved the phone away from his mouth so he could speak to Robin. "My mom doesn't have any hot water. Zach needs my help. We may have to install a new hot water heater for her."

"Go help your brother. I'll be fine."

Brent frowned. "I won't leave you alone, not until Holden is caught."

"Brent, you live in a very secure complex. I'll lock the door as soon as you leave and won't open it for anyone."

That should be enough to satisfy Brent, but it wasn't. "No." He placed the phone next to his mouth again. "Can Michelle come over until we're through? I'd feel better if someone stayed with Robin."

"She left with the three guys this morning for the coast. They'll be back Tuesday."

"Shit," Brent muttered.

"Brent, I'll be fine," Robin said. "Take care of your mother."

"What about Breanna?" Zach asked. "She's here. She came over to have breakfast with us."

Brent doubted if Breanna would be any help in shooing away a fly, but at least Robin wouldn't be alone. "Yeah, okay."

"Great. We'll be there about ten."

"Bring breakfast with you. Robin wanted omelets and I won't have time to fix them."

"No problem. I'll have Jade make up a couple of to-go plates. See you at ten."

Brent closed his phone and laid it on the nightstand. "Breanna's coming over with Zach to stay with you while I'm gone." He wrapped his arms around Robin's waist. "Sorry. I'll fix omelets tomorrow morning."

"I'm going to need more clothes before tomorrow. Breanna can ride over to my house with me to—"

"No," he said firmly. "You do not leave this condo without me."

"Brent, I'm not a child."

"I know that, but I'll feel a lot better if you're here behind locked doors. I want Holden behind bars where he belongs before you go out by yourself." He moved his hands to her face, cradling her jaw. "Promise me you won't leave, okay?"

Robin kissed him softly. "I promise."

Chapter Seventeen

Robin looked up from her laptop keys when she heard the doorbell. She started to rise from the dining room table to answer it as Brent stepped out of the kitchen. One stern look from him stopped her.

"I'll get it."

"It's probably Zach and Breanna."

"We don't know that for sure. You stay there."

Protection was one thing, but Robin refused to hide in the dining room while Brent opened the door. She followed him into the living room, standing by the end of the couch to give her a clear view of the door. Breanna crossed the threshold, followed by Zach. Breanna waved at Robin and smiled.

"Hi! Ready to go shopping?"

Brent closed the door and scowled. "No shopping. You and Robin aren't leaving here for anything."

"I was teasing. Lighten up, unc."

Shaking his head, Brent looked at his brother. "You had to marry a woman with a brat for a daughter."

Breanna patted Brent's cheek. "You love me and you know it." She flounced by him and walked to Robin. "Don't let him give you a hard time. He's all bark and no bite."

"Actually," Robin said, her gaze on Brent, "his bite is very sexy."

"Ewww." Breanna wrinkled her nose. "That's too much information, Robin."

"I think we should leave now," Zach said.

"I agree." Brent picked up his jacket from the back of the couch. "Lock the chain and the deadbolt as soon as we leave."

Robin joined him at the door. Brent stepped outside, then turned and dropped a soft kiss on her lips. "Do *not* open this door for anyone, okay?"

"I won't."

"I'll call you when we're on our way back."

"Okay. Be careful."

He ran one finger across her jaw. Her throat tightened at the tenderness in his eyes. "I don't want to leave you," he whispered.

Robin smiled. "I'll be fine."

He didn't look convinced. Robin clasped the lapels of his jacket and pulled him down for another kiss. "Hurry back."

After she shut and locked the door as per Brent's instructions, she turned to face Breanna, who held out a foil-wrapped package.

"Breakfast from Mom. A biscuit sandwich with ham and cheese. Nice and fattening and nummy. And…" She reached into her tote and pulled out a plastic container. "Mom's special spiced tea. Guaranteed to warm you up no matter how cold you are."

"Sounds perfect."

"You start your breakfast. I'll heat up water for the tea."

Robin returned to her chair at the dining room table and unwrapped her sandwich. Her stomach growled at the aroma of ham and cheese. She took a huge bite, and rolled her eyes from pleasure. She could quickly get addicted to Jade's cooking.

No one had ever cared for her or taken care of her the way everyone in the Cooper family had done. Breanna didn't have to give up her Sunday morning to be here, yet she had.

"That kitchen is way too big for a single guy." Brenna sat in the chair across from Robin. "I finally found a tea kettle. The water will be hot in a minute."

Laying her half-eaten sandwich on the foil, Robin wiped her hands on a napkin. "Thank you for coming over today."

Breanna shrugged one shoulder. "No problem. I brought my books with me. I'll curl up on the couch and study so I won't be in your way."

"Do you graduate soon?"

"May. I made a deal with Mom to take a year off and do some traveling before I start law school." She grinned. "I want to check out the nude beaches in Europe."

"Sounds like a good deal to me."

"Michelle had planned to go with me, until she got involved with Andre and Nathan. Now she doesn't look at any guys but them. What a waste."

"They're very handsome."

"And sexy. And I know she loves them. But I was really looking forward to her going with me."

A loud whistle came from the kitchen. "Water's ready," Breanna said. "I'll get our tea."

Robin clicked a few keys on her laptop and added a graphic to her client's website. The mess with Stuart, plus all the time she'd spent with Brent, had put her behind schedule. She prided herself on her guarantee that changes would be made within twenty-four hours. These changes should've been completed two days ago. Luckily, her client hadn't expected her to work over the Thanksgiving holiday weekend.

Breanna came back a few moments later with two mugs of tea. She handed one to Robin and took her chair again. "So, what are you working on?"

"A client's website. I'm doing some updates."

"Do you like what you do?"

"Very much. I like using my imagination, being creative. Although my creative juices don't seem to be running very quickly today."

Sympathy filled Breanna's eyes. "You've gone through a lot lately."

"It certainly hasn't been fun."

Breanna placed her elbows on the table and held her mug with both hands. "Zach told me the police don't have any leads."

"Not yet. Detective Stone thinks Stuart is somehow connected to Coopers' Companions. I don't know how that could be possible. I looked at pictures of all the escorts. Stuart isn't one of them."

"Maybe his appearance has changed over the years."

"That's what the detective said, but I'm sure Stuart isn't one of the escorts. He couldn't have changed *that* much. I know I'd recognize Stuart if I saw him."

"Is he handsome?"

"Very. Or he was. I don't know what he looks like now."

"Do you have a picture of him?"

Robin shook her head. "No. Detective Stone asked me the same thing. I threw away anything to do with Stuart when I left Colorado."

"I have an insatiable curiosity. I really want to know what he looks like." She tapped the lid of Robin's laptop. "What about online? Was his picture in the newspaper when he was arrested?"

Robin hadn't considered looking at the online newspapers. "It was, but I don't know if the article about Stuart will be online. That was eight years ago."

"There's one way to find out."

Breanna rounded the table and slipped into the chair next to Robin as Robin did a search for the Denver newspapers. After calling up the home pages and checking the links, she found the one for archived stories. Unfortunately, only the articles were kept, no pictures.

"Struck out again," Breanna said with a sigh.

A tinkling bell sound came from Robin's computer. "What's that?" Breanna asked.

"I have new email. I'll check it later."

"Go ahead and check it now." She drained her mug. "Do you want more tea?"

"Yes, please."

Robin clicked the icon to open her email program. She saw two new messages from clients, and one from Evan Stone that included an attachment. She immediately opened his message.

Robin,

Briggins sent this picture of Holden. Show it to Brent and Zach and see if they recognize him.

I'll keep you posted on any developments.

Evan.

She scrolled down to see the attachment. Chills raced down her spine when the picture of Stuart filled her screen. She'd never imagined he would come back into her life once he went to prison.

"Anything important?" Breanna asked, holding out a fresh mug of tea to Robin.

"You're in luck. You wanted to see a picture of Stuart. Detective Stone just sent me one."

Breanna slid onto her chair and peered at Stuart's picture. "Damn. He is a hunk, even in that mug shot. I wouldn't forget a face like that." She sipped her tea, her gaze still fastened to the laptop screen. A frown drew her eyebrows together. "It's funny. I would swear I've seen him." She tapped one long fingernail against her teeth. "Not at school. Not at work." She leaned closer to the screen and narrowed her eyes. "Can you print out the picture so I can get a better look at it?"

"Sure. Brent turned on his printer for me this morning so I could connect to it."

"Where is it?"

"In his bedroom. End of the hall."

Robin pressed the command to print as Breanna left the room. She came back moments later with a piece of paper bearing Stuart's likeness. She continued to frown as she studied the picture.

"He doesn't have a mustache now. And his hair is different. It's short, almost military short. I can see his face so clearly, but I can't figure out where…"

Breanna stopped. Her eyes widened, her mouth dropped open. "My God." She looked at Robin. "I know who he is."

* * * * *

Robin tapped her foot as she waited for Detective Stone to answer his phone. She couldn't believe what Breanna had told her about Stuart. He was *here*, right here in Fort Worth, only a few miles away.

"What's happening?" Breanna asked.

Robin held up one finger to silence Breanna when she heard Evan's voicemail message. "Damn it," she muttered. She didn't want to leave a message. She wanted to talk to the detective *now*.

"Detective Stone, this is Robin Howell. I think I know where Stuart is. Please call me back on my cell, 555-9811."

She shut her cell phone and slipped it into her slacks pocket. "I got his voice mail."

"Well, hell." Breanna paced away a few steps, then turned and walked back to Robin. "Now what?"

"We wait for him to call back."

"Forget that. I don't wait well." Breanna tapped one fingernail against her teeth again. Suddenly, her eyes widened and she smiled. "I know! We can go and check out Stuart ourselves."

She couldn't believe Breanna would suggest such a dangerous thing. "No we can't. That would be incredibly stupid. We're talking about the man who set my house on fire with me in it."

Breanna frowned. "I can't just sit and wait for some dumb man to get back to me. I don't need to be escorted by a police detective." She held out her hand to Robin, palm up. "Give me your car keys."

"What?"

"I'm going to check out Stuart."

"No you aren't. We wait, Breanna. Detective Stone will call soon. And besides, Brent and Zach will be back any minute."

"Fine. You don't want to give me your keys? I'll find the keys to Brent's car. They're probably in his bedroom."

Breanna made it three steps before Robin grabbed her arm to stop her. "You can't take Brent's car without asking him."

"Then let's go in yours. I'll drive."

Robin hesitated, torn between waiting to talk to Detective Stone and seeing for herself if Stuart was actually the man Breanna knew. "I promised Brent I wouldn't leave his condo."

"I'm going, with or without you, even if I have to call a cab." Breanna reached into Robin's slacks pocket and pulled out the cell phone. "Call Brent. Tell him what I told you."

She could do that. As long as she checked with Brent, she wouldn't be breaking her promise to stay put.

Four rings later, the call went to voicemail. "Damn it! Why can't these guys answer their phones?"

"Voicemail?"

"Yeah." She waited for the tone. "Brent, it's Robin. Breanna thinks she knows who Stuart is. She's determined to go and find out, and I won't let her go by herself. I promise we'll be careful."

She closed her phone and slipped it back in her pocket. "Let's go."

* * * * *

"Thanks again," Colleen called out from her front porch.

"Anytime." Brent placed the toolbox in the bed of Zach's pickup, then waved at his mother. "See you later."

He climbed into the passenger seat as Zach started the motor. "At least she didn't need a new water heater."

"Yet. Her heater is at least seven years old. We probably should replace it before it goes out."

"I agree."

"You want me to stop and pick up lunch?"

"I'll call Robin and see if that's okay with her or if she'd rather go out."

Zach chuckled. "Man, you do have it bad."

"Shut up, Zach."

"I think it's great. I really like Robin." He reached over and playfully socked Brent's arm. "Y'all make such a cute couple."

"Shut *up*, Zach."

Brent reached for the cell phone on his belt. It wasn't there. "Oh hell. I've lost my phone."

"Want me to go back to Mom's? You probably dropped it in her house."

"Or in her yard, or the parking lot at home, or the hardware store. Damn it!"

"Here." Zach unclipped his phone from his belt and handed it to Brent. "Use mine to call Robin."

"Thanks."

Brent frowned when he heard Robin's voicemail message. "That's weird. It went to her voicemail."

"Maybe she didn't hear her phone ring. Or she's talking to someone."

"Yeah, maybe." A knot formed in his stomach. His frown deepened. "I don't like this."

"I'm sure the gals are fine."

"You may be sure, but I'm not. I'm gonna try Breanna's number. Do you have it?"

"Yeah. It's programmed in."

The knot in Brent's stomach tightened when he got Breanna's voice mail too. "Shit!" He shut Zach's phone with a loud snap. "Something's wrong, Zach. Damn it, I knew I shouldn't have left Robin."

Brent's hand shook as he punched in Robin's cell number again. If Stuart had gotten to Robin, if he'd hurt her in any way, Brent would kill the bastard without a moment of remorse.

* * * * *

Robin's car was gone.

Brent's heart dropped to his feet. "Why the *hell* would they leave? Robin promised me she wouldn't go anywhere."

"They probably went shopping or to a movie."

"Yeah, and it was probably Breanna's idea. I'm going to wring her neck. I told Robin not to leave the condo."

Brent barely waited for Zach to park the pickup before he jumped from the cab and ran toward the outside stairs. He bounded up the stairs, quickly unlocked the door to his condo and pushed it open. "Robin! Robin, where are you?"

Silence. He hurried down the hall and checked the bedrooms and bathrooms. By the time he made it back to the living room, Zach had entered the condo.

"Any luck?" Zach asked.

"No. I'm gonna check the kitchen."

The kitchen was empty, the tea kettle on the stove and two mugs in the sink the only evidence the women had been there.

"Brent!" Zach called out.

Brent hurried into the dining room to find Zach standing by the table, holding out a piece of paper. "Look at this."

Brent took the paper and stared at the image. "Fuck," he muttered. "Holden has been under our nose the whole time." He looked back at Zach. "Where did you get this?"

"I found it on the table. I checked Robin's computer. Looks like Stone sent the picture to her this morning in an email."

"Breanna must have recognized him."

"And knowing my stepdaughter, she decided to go have a look at him to be sure."

"I *am* going to wring her neck, Zach."

"Get in line after me."

Brent tossed the picture back on the table. "I'll call Stone on the way. Let's go."

Chapter Eighteen

ಐ

Robin stopped inside the doorway to let her eyes adjust to the dim lighting. She wiped her sweaty palms on her thighs. She only had to take a quick look to be sure Stuart was here. She didn't have to talk to him, she didn't have to get close to him. He wouldn't be able to hurt her in a public place.

That knowledge didn't stop the fear from creeping up her spine.

"There's a table in the corner," Breanna said. "That'll give us a good view of the whole room."

Several of the tables were occupied by men. Robin noticed them watching her and Breanna as they walked past. A few nodded, some smiled, before switching their attention back to the football game on the big screen TVs.

"Zach and Brent come here all the time," Breanna said. "I came with them and Mom a couple of times. The food is really good."

Robin couldn't imagine trying to eat anything now. She removed a menu from between the paper napkin holder and the salt shaker to make it look as if she planned to order lunch. A large graphic of different sports balls covered the front, with the words First and Ten in bold letters bursting from the balls.

Stuart, a bartender in a sports bar. She had a hard time believing that.

A lovely redhead approached their table, wearing a name badge that said *Nikki*. "Hi, ladies. What can I get you to drink?"

"A plain Coke for me. Robin?"

"That's fine."

"Coming right up," Nikki said with a smile.

"Is Trey here today?" Breanna asked.

"No, he's off today and tomorrow."

"Too bad." Breanna grinned wickedly. "He's really nice to look at."

"He certainly is." The waitress smiled again. "I'll be right back with your drinks."

As soon as Nikki walked away, Breanna's smile faded. "*Damn* it."

Robin agreed with that. She wanted this whole thing to be over. If she could see this Trey, know for certain that he was the man Breanna claimed was Stuart, she'd feel as if her nightmare was about to end. "It was a good try. We'll wait for Detective Stone and Brent to call, and go from there."

"I told you, I'm not good with waiting." Breanna drummed her fingernails on the table. "There has to be something we can do."

"Like what? Drive up to Stuart's house and knock on his door?"

As soon as the words were out of her mouth, she saw the light bulb go off behind Breanna's eyes. "You can't be thinking what I think you're thinking."

"All we need is his address."

"Breanna, that's crazy! Even if we had his address, we can't go to his house. Stuart is a killer."

"Don't you want to know for sure that Trey is Stuart?"

"Of course I do."

"Then a little drive-by will be perfect."

"And how do you propose we get his address? I doubt if the manager here will turn it over to us."

"I'll think of something." She looked past Robin, her eyebrows drawn together in a frown. Suddenly, her frown disappeared and she stood. "I'll be right back."

"Where are you going?"

"Ladies' room."

Nikki brought their drinks after Breanna left. Robin declined Nikki's offer to take a lunch order, saying she'd rather wait until her friend returned.

The waitress had barely walked away when Breanna came back. She tossed a ten-dollar bill on the table and grabbed her jacket from the back of the chair. "Let's go."

"Go? Why?"

Breanna gave her a look that clearly said to obey her and not ask questions. Robin took one fast sip of her drink, then picked up her own jacket and followed Breanna from the bar.

She waited until they were back in her car with Breanna behind the wheel before speaking again. "Why the fast getaway?"

"I saw an office in the hallway next to the restrooms the last time I was here. I took a chance that it might be unlocked. It was." She reached in the pocket of her jeans and handed Robin a piece of paper. "Trey's address."

"How did you get this?"

"Sneakiness and cunning."

Robin decided Breanna was a good person to have on her side. "Do you know where this is?"

"Yeah. It isn't far from here."

"You might as well keep driving once we verify Trey is really Stuart. If we go back, Brent will strangle both of us."

"Not if we find Stuart."

"Do you have a plan?"

"Not...exactly. But I'll think of something."

* * * * *

Brent stepped down from Zach's pickup as Evan climbed out of his car. Evan had pulled into the parking lot of First and Ten only seconds after Brent and Zach arrived.

"They aren't here," Brent told the detective. "I don't see Robin's car. Shit! Why didn't you answer your goddamned phone when she called you?"

"I don't take my cell in the shower with me."

Brent wanted to punch Stone for sounding so calm. "So what the hell are we supposed to do?"

"The first thing *you* have to do is calm down. We'll go in the bar and find out if they were here. And *I* do the talking. Got it?"

"Yeah, yeah, you do the talking."

Evan led the way into the bar. A flash of his badge and the manager on duty was only too happy to cooperate. He not only gave them Trey's address and phone number but, after speaking with Nikki, verified that Robin and Breanna had left less than fifteen minutes earlier.

Once outside again, Evan turned toward his car. "I'll call this in, then head to Holden's house."

"Wait a minute, " Brent said. "You aren't going anywhere without us."

"This is a police matter, Brent. I'll handle it."

"Fuck that. I'm not going home to sit and wait until someone decides to call me."

"Stone, Breanna is my stepdaughter. I need to know she's okay."

Evan frowned. "I'll have backup. We'll make sure Robin and Breanna are okay."

"No arguments, Stone. Zach and I are going. That's final."

Evan looked from one man to the other. "I can't stop you if you decide to go for a drive in Holden's neighborhood." He slid into his car and lowered the window. "Don't interfere."

"No problem."

* * * * *

The county road was little more than one lane wide with houses spaced a quarter to half a mile apart. Robin wondered why Stuart had chosen such a deserted place to live. He'd always wanted to be in the middle of the city, to be close to the action.

Maybe Stuart and Trey weren't the same person after all.

Breanna turned around and drove by the small white house again. She'd had no trouble finding the address. "The garage is closed. There's no way to tell if he's home."

Disappointment curled inside Robin's stomach. She'd thought Breanna was crazy to suggest they simply drive to Trey's house. Now that they were here, she longed to know the truth...if Trey Dutton and Stuart Holden were the same person. "We can't knock on his front door, that's for sure."

Breanna touched the brake and stopped the car. "Why not?"

"Okay, now I *know* you're crazy. We can't go to his front door."

"No, *we* can't, but *I* can." Eyes wide with excitement, Breanna grabbed Robin's arm. "That's perfect! I'll knock on the door and pretend I'm lost. You can hunker down in the seat so he can't see you, but you can see him and ID him."

It sounded logical, which meant there had to be something wrong with the plan. It couldn't be that easy.

Breanna touched the gas and turned the car around a third time. "Let's do it."

She pulled into the driveway and parked in front of the closed garage door. "You shouldn't have any problem seeing his face from here."

Robin slid down in the seat. Tugging her jacket over her head, she peeked through the opening as Breanna walked up on the porch and knocked on the door. Several moments passed before the door opened. She saw Breanna smile and speak, but she couldn't see who had answered the door for he or she stood in the shadows.

Step out! I need to see your face.

Whoever had answered the door grabbed Breanna's arm and spun her around. Both her arms were jammed up between her shoulder blades. A long, thin knife was pressed to her throat. She took two steps forward, until the person holding her appeared in the doorway.

Stuart.

He looked different with his short hair and clean-shaven face, but he was every bit as handsome as she remembered. There'd been a time when she'd lived for a smile from him. He'd killed all her feelings with his possessiveness and jealousy.

"Get out of the car, Robin," he called out.

Robin dropped her jacket and opened the door. Her legs shook. She had to hold onto the car door a moment before she could stand on her own.

"Come here."

His command plus the fear in Breanna's eyes urged Robin to make her legs work. She walked across the yard and slowly climbed the two steps to the porch. Stuart backed into the house, dragging Breanna with him.

"Close the door," he commanded once Robin stepped across the threshold.

She did. "How did you know I was in the car?"

He laughed, an evil sound that turned her blood cold. "Don't you think I know your car? If you wanted to sneak up on me, you should've driven something else."

She stared at the knife against Breanna's throat. "Please don't hurt her."

"You aren't in any position to tell me what to do." He jerked Breanna's arms upward. She cried out in pain.

"Stuart, stop it! Let her go. You want me, not her."

He dragged Breanna farther inside the house. Robin followed. He stopped when they reached the kitchen at the back of the house.

"We can't take the chance of anyone seeing inside the living room windows, now can we?"

He pressed the knife higher against Breanna's throat. She rose to her tiptoes and winced. A drop of blood appeared next to the knife. Tears filled Breanna's eyes.

"Stuart, please let her go."

"You spoiled my plans, Robin. I wasn't ready for you to find me. I wanted to play with you longer, make you suffer the way I suffered."

She had to keep him talking so he wouldn't hurt Breanna. "I'm sorry."

"Are you? Or are you playing with me?"

"What do you want me to do?"

"I want you to be with me forever, the way we planned."

"Okay. Fine. We can do that. Let Breanna go and we'll talk about it."

His eyes narrowed, his lips tightened. "Don't fuck with me, Robin."

"I'm not! I'll do whatever you want. Just let Breanna go."

He gripped the knife tighter. "I don't think so. I think you need to be taught a lesson. Watching while I cut nice long strips into your friend's skin will be a good punishment for you."

Breanna squeezed her eyes closed. Tears seeped beneath the lids to roll down her cheeks. Robin knew Breanna had to be scared out of her mind.

Stuart moved the knife and nicked Breanna's neck. She gasped. A thin stream of blood ran down to stain the neckline of her T-shirt.

"Stuart, stop it!"

The enjoyment in his eyes sickened her. "What's wrong, Robin? You don't like the sight of blood?"

"Please let her go, Stuart. I promise I'll do whatever you want."

Breanna opened her eyes again. Her gaze darted about the room. She froze for a second before looking back at Robin. Her gaze cut to her right again. Robin assumed Breanna was trying to show her something, but she was afraid to look away from Stuart in case he became suspicious.

She lowered her head and rubbed her forehead with one hand to hide her eyes from Stuart. Looking in the direction Breanna had indicated, she saw a drainer of dishes on the cabinet only two feet from her. A large skillet lay on the top. If she or Breanna could somehow distract Stuart long enough for her to grab that skillet...

She looked back at her friend. Breanna gave a slight nod, indicating she was ready. "Now!" Robin said.

Breanna rammed the back of her head into Stuart's nose.

"Shit!" he roared.

Blood poured from his nose. His hand with the knife fell away from Breanna's neck. Robin didn't give him the chance to regroup. Grabbing the handle with both hands, she swung the skillet as hard as she could at Stuart's head. His eyes rolled back and he fell to his hands and knees. The knife skittered across the tile floor.

Robin raised the skillet to hit Stuart again when the back door flew open. Evan dropped to one knee, his pistol held straight in front of him.

"Police!"

Two uniformed officers hurried into the room, guns also drawn. Robin dropped the skillet and grabbed Breanna, pulling her out of the way of the officers.

Evan walked over to the two women as the officers cuffed Stuart and dragged him to his feet. "Are you all right?"

Robin nodded. "We're fine."

His gaze snapped to Breanna's neck. He scowled. "Did he cut you?"

She touched the nick on her neck. "A little. I'm okay."

Evan looked from one woman to the other. "I don't know whether to praise you for your bravery, or tell you how stupid you are to come here on your own."

"Robin!"

She turned at the sound of Brent's voice. Before she could draw a breath to speak to him, he grabbed her in a fierce hug and lifted her off her feet.

"Thank God you're all right." Setting her back on her feet, he squeezed her again. "I was so scared." He drew back and looked into her eyes, a thunderous scowl on his face. "And furious. What the hell were you thinking, going after Holden on your own?"

"Don't yell at her, Brent," Breanna said, pulling out of Zach's arms. "I convinced Robin we should try to find out if Trey and Stuart were the same man."

Zach kissed the top of Breanna's head. "Y'all are safe and Holden has been captured. That's all that matters."

Evan approached the foursome. He looked at Robin. "I'll need a statement from you and Breanna."

"Jesus, Stone," Brent said, his scowl deepening. "Can't you do that another time? Robin has been through enough today."

"No, it's okay." Robin gave Brent a soft kiss. "I want to do it now and get it over with. Breanna needs medical help first–"

"I don't need any medical help. It's just a nick. I can give my statement now."

"Are you sure you don't want me to take you to the hospital?" Zach asked.

"No, I don't want you to take me to the hospital. I feel the same way Robin does. Let's get this whole thing over with."

"Okay," Evan said. "I'll lead the way to the station."

Chapter Nineteen

Robin snuggled her face into Brent's pillow. He'd ushered her into his bedroom, told her to get naked and lie on her stomach on his bed. When she asked him why, he'd smiled mysteriously and shut the door, leaving her alone in the room.

Closing her eyes, she released a sigh and thought about today's events. All of them merged into one big blur—seeing Stuart, his capture, giving her statement to Evan. By the time she left the police station, she was completely drained and ready to collapse.

Zach invited everyone to his house for an early dinner. No one had eaten lunch, so he didn't receive any arguments. Robin didn't know how Jade managed to cook since she kept Breanna right by her side the whole time. Breanna had acted all brave and fearless, until she'd seen her mother. Then she'd broken down and sobbed in Jade's arms.

Robin would've done the same thing if she had a mother.

The warm hug she'd received from Colleen had helped. Michelle and the three guys had turned around and come back as soon as Zach called her. Robin had received hugs from all of them. Everyone in the Cooper family treated her as if she were one of their own.

She appreciated their love and caring, but she wanted love from the one Cooper who couldn't give it to her.

Now that Stuart had been caught, she'd go back to her house and Brent would go back to his regular life as an escort. She didn't expect a declaration of love from him, although she yearned to hear it. The three little words lived on the tip of her tongue. She wanted so much to tell him of her feelings, yet wouldn't. Brent wasn't a happily-ever-after guy. She'd known that ever since she met him.

She'd spend one more night in his arms, then return to her life tomorrow.

The bedroom door opened. Robin rose to her elbows to look over her shoulder, but stopped at Brent's words.

"Don't move. Just stay comfortable."

"Where have you been? My butt is cold."

"It won't be for long. Lie down."

She snuggled into the pillow again. She heard different noises as Brent moved around the room— the rustle of a paper sack, the strike of a match, the rattle of his belt buckle.

"What are you doing?"

"I've told you that you're entirely too impatient." She heard the click of the bedside lamp as Brent turned it off. The bed dipped. A flip-top opened. "I promised you something three days ago and it's time I delivered."

He picked up her left foot with his warm, oil-covered hands. They slid over her skin, his thumbs gently caressing. Robin released a contented sigh. "That's nice."

"You haven't lived until you've had one of my massages."

She inhaled deeply of the scent of lavender and vanilla. "Is the oil lavender?"

"Yeah. Michelle told me that's the most calming scent. The candles are vanilla. She gave me those too."

"She's very handy to have around."

"Sometimes. Most of the time she's a pain in the ass."

"I know how much you love her."

"Yeah, I do." He switched to her right foot. "That doesn't mean she isn't a pain in the ass."

Robin chuckled, then moaned when Brent slid his hands over her calf. "You're going to turn me into mush."

"Good. That's what I want." He switched to her other calf. "I was really scared today, Robin," he said softly.

The way he'd grabbed her, held her, at Stuart's house proved that. "I know."

"If you didn't have such a luscious ass, I'd paddle it for leaving this condo when you promised me you wouldn't." His hands moved up her thighs, his thumbs digging into the muscles. "Don't ever do anything like that again, okay?"

"I won't have to. Stuart is in jail where he belongs."

Brent poured oil directly onto her low back. "I talked to Stone while I was gone. He had a long talk with Holden. He told Stone about his housemate—Jim Bradshaw."

That name sounded familiar to Robin, but she couldn't figure out why. "Should I know him?"

"He's one of our escorts. Holden admitted he read Jim's email. That's how he found out when you'd be at the office taking pictures." His thumbs pressed beneath her shoulder blades. "He's a master on the computer. He's tracked you ever since he went to prison, with help from his cousin."

"His cousin?"

"You didn't know his cousin is his attorney?"

"No. I had no idea."

"The cousin used his contacts to follow you every time you moved and he'd report to Holden. The bastard knew everything about you, Robin. Stone found a thick folder in Jim's house with all kinds of information, including your credit card numbers. He tracked everything you did."

She'd been violated for years and never knew about it. Robin shivered.

Brent kissed her softly between her shoulder blades. "I'm sorry. I shouldn't have told you that."

"I'm glad you did. I want to know everything."

"You know enough for now. This massage is supposed to relax you. I can feel your shoulders tightening up again." He slipped between her legs on his knees. "Maybe I need to do more to relax you."

She felt his semi-hard cock brush her buttocks. Her pussy clenched with the need to have him inside her. She could lift her hips in invitation and he'd slide into her sheath. It was a delicious thought, but she wanted more. If this was their last night together, she wanted everything.

Robin moved far enough away from him until she could turn around. She rose to her knees and faced him. His gaze dipped to her breasts, her mound, before he looked into her eyes again. "What are you doing? I didn't finish your massage."

"I have another idea."

"Will it relax you?"

"It'll melt my bones."

His mouth tipped up on one side in his crooked grin. "Then go for it."

Pushing Brent to his back, she leaned over and covered his mouth with hers. She cradled his jaw, rubbing his cheek with her thumb as she kissed him. She caressed his lips with hers, slowly, gently, in no hurry to stop.

He slid one hand up and down her back and over her buttock. Robin traced his lips with the tip of her tongue, nipped at the pounding pulse in his neck.

A deep growl came from his throat.

She traveled down his body, dropping soft kisses. She whisked her tongue over each nipple, bit the firm muscle of his breast, then continued down his body. The soft hair tickled her lips. She licked and nibbled his stomach, darted her tongue into his navel.

"Robin." His voice came out low and guttural.

Gripping the base of his cock, she ran her tongue around the head. She slid her mouth down his length and back to the tip. One more circle of the head and she took him in her mouth again. She sucked hard as she moved her lips up and down his cock.

Brent tunneled the fingers of one hand into her hair. "Damn, you are really good at that."

Robin licked one finger and slid it beneath his balls to tickle his anus. His hand fisted in her hair. "You need to stop before I come."

Ignoring him, Robin continued to move her mouth up and down his shaft. She pushed her wet finger inside his ass. Brent groaned loudly and spread his legs.

"Oh yeah. Go deeper, babe."

Robin added a second finger, pushing them as far inside his ass as she could reach. Brent's body jerked. He arched his hips and squeezed his eyes closed. His warm semen hit the back of her throat. Robin greedily swallowed every drop.

She rose to her knees between his splayed legs. She could see the pulse pounding in his neck, could hear his heavy breathing. Slowly he opened his eyes and looked at her. Despite his climax, his eyes still burned with desire. Robin was already wet. The look in his eyes made her channel flood with more moisture.

Brent moved until his head rested on a pillow at the head of the bed. He touched his mouth. "I want your pussy right here."

Robin climbed up his body and did as he commanded. Gripping her buttocks, he ran his tongue from anus to clit. She clutched the headboard and closed her eyes. He gently pulled her feminine lips with his teeth, then licked her clit again.

That talented tongue flashed over her clit, dove into her sheath. She began to move her hips back and forth, riding his tongue. She moved for several moments before he gripped her buttocks tighter and held her against his mouth. He licked her entire labia, then suckled her clit.

It took mere moments for the direct stimulation on those sensitive nerves to push her over the edge. A keening moan ripped from her throat when the pleasure galloped up from her toes to envelop her body.

She didn't have the chance to catch her breath before Brent tugged her down to straddle his hips. Her labia cushioned his hard cock. He hissed.

"*God*, that feels good."

Something else would feel even better. Robin rose to her knees, clasped his shaft at the base and impaled herself.

"Yeah. I love how hot and wet your pussy gets." He cradled her breasts and thumbed her nipples to stiff peaks. "Ride me."

She propped her hands on his shoulders and lifted her hips until only the head of his cock remained inside her. She slowly lowered herself to take all of him again. Her movements were easy at first, but soon gained speed as her desire grew.

He gripped her waist and thrust into her. "I want to feel that beautiful pussy grab my cock. Come for me, babe. I love to feel you come."

"Ohhhhhhhhhhh." Robin threw back her head and arched her back. The walls of her pussy convulsed, milking his shaft as she came. Brent gripped her waist tighter and continued to thrust into her for several moments until he groaned out his own release.

She wilted onto his chest. Brent wrapped his arms around her tightly and brushed his lips across the top of her head. "Did your bones melt?" he asked.

"Totally."

"So did mine. I don't normally come twice in such a short amount of time."

"Me either."

Content to hold her, Brent lay still and caressed her back while her breathing and heartbeat slowed to normal. He'd never thought he could feel so deeply for a woman. One short week ago, he'd been happy with his life, happy to bed a different woman every week. Now he couldn't imagine making love with anyone but Robin.

She filled his heart, his soul.

His life.

Brent kissed the top of her head again. "You're going to have to work on Coopers' Companions website again tomorrow."

"I can't do much more until I get the rest of the guys' pictures."

"You need to take down my profile."

"Why?"

"Because I'm no longer an escort."

She lifted her head and looked at him. "Why?"

"I can't see any other women when I'm in love with you."

"In love…" She stopped and her eyes widened. "What?"

Brent smiled and pushed her hair back from her face. "You sound shocked."

"You love me?"

"Is that so hard to believe?"

"But I thought you were happy being Coopers' Companions' number one guy."

"I was, until I met you."

Words had always been easy for Brent. He knew what to say to make a woman feel good, or put her in the mood for sex. Now, when he needed to tell Robin how much she meant to him, he wasn't sure which words to use.

He looked into her eyes and knew exactly what to say.

"You turned my whole world upside down. It pissed me off at first, I'll admit that. But now…" His gaze passed over her hair, her face. "You're more precious to me than anyone in my life."

Tears filled her eyes. Her fingers trembled as she touched his lips. "I love you too."

Brent kissed her tenderly. Holding her tightly to him, he rolled them over so he lay on top of her, their bodies still intimately joined. His cock began to stir again. "I have an idea."

Robin grinned impishly. "Yeah, I can feel your 'idea'."

He chuckled. "Not that. Well, not yet. I bought a decadent chocolate dessert for us. I thought we could…" He kissed the tip of her nose. "Have dessert, then…" Her jaw. "Relax in the hot tub, then…" The area behind her ear. "Make love again." He kissed her lips once more. "What do you think?"

Robin smiled. "I think you have wonderful ideas."

The End

Also by Lynn LaFleur

☙

A Cupid's Work is Never Done
Capsized
Candy Caresses (*anthology*)
Coopers' Companions 1: Rent-A-Stud
Coopers' Companions 2: Michelle's Men
Ellora's Cavemen: Legendary Tails I (*anthology*)
Ellora's Cavemen: Seasons of Seduction IV (*anthology*)
Enchanted Rogues (*anthology*)
Happy Birthday, Baby
Holiday Heat (*anthology*)
Naughty Nooners: Door Prize
One Night of Pleasure
Premonition
Two Men and a Lady (*anthology*)
White Hot Holidays Vol. 2 (*anthology*)

About the Author

Lynn LaFleur was born and raised in a small town in Texas close to the Dallas/Fort Worth area. Writing has been in her blood since she was eight years old and wrote her first "story" for an English assignment.

As well as writing at every possible moment, Lynn enjoys reading, scrapbooking, photography, and learning new things on the computer. She's a software junky and loves to try out new programs, especially anything to do with graphics.

After living on the West Coast for 21 years, Lynn now lives 17 miles from her hometown in Texas. She's a romantic at heart and can't imagine ever writing anything but romances. A full-time writer, she spends her days creating stories of people who find their happily-ever-after, sometimes with the help of an alien or psychic or vampire.

Lynn welcomes comments from readers. You can find her website and email address on her author bio page at www.ellorascave.com.

Tell Us What You Think

We appreciate hearing reader opinions about our books. You can email us at Comments@EllorasCave.com.

Why an electronic book?

We live in the Information Age—an exciting time in the history of human civilization, in which technology rules supreme and continues to progress in leaps and bounds every minute of every day. For a multitude of reasons, more and more avid literary fans are opting to purchase e-books instead of paper books. The question from those not yet initiated into the world of electronic reading is simply: *Why?*

1. ***Price.*** An electronic title at Ellora's Cave Publishing and Cerridwen Press runs anywhere from 40% to 75% less than the cover price of the exact same title in paperback format. Why? Basic mathematics and cost. It is less expensive to publish an e-book (no paper and printing, no warehousing and shipping) than it is to publish a paperback, so the savings are passed along to the consumer.

2. ***Space.*** Running out of room in your house for your books? That is one worry you will never have with electronic books. For a low one-time cost, you can purchase a handheld device specifically designed for e-reading. Many e-readers have large, convenient screens for viewing. Better yet, hundreds of titles can be stored within your new library—on a single microchip. There are a variety of e-readers from different manufacturers. You can also read e-books on your PC or laptop computer. (Please note that Ellora's Cave does not endorse any specific brands.)

You can check our websites at www.ellorascave.com or www.cerridwenpress.com for information we make available to new consumers.)

3. ***Mobility.*** Because your new e-library consists of only a microchip within a small, easily transportable e-reader, your entire cache of books can be taken with you wherever you go.

4. ***Personal Viewing Preferences.*** Are the words you are currently reading too small? Too large? Too... ANNOYING? Paperback books cannot be modified according to personal preferences, but e-books can.

5. ***Instant Gratification.*** Is it the middle of the night and all the bookstores near you are closed? Are you tired of waiting days, sometimes weeks, for bookstores to ship the novels you bought? Ellora's Cave Publishing sells instantaneous downloads twenty-four hours a day, seven days a week, every day of the year. Our webstore is never closed. Our e-book delivery system is 100% automated, meaning your order is filled as soon as you pay for it.

Those are a few of the top reasons why electronic books are replacing paperbacks for many avid readers.

As always, Ellora's Cave and Cerridwen Press welcome your questions and comments. We invite you to email us at Comments@ellorascave.com or write to us directly at Ellora's Cave Publishing Inc., 1056 Home Avenue, Akron, OH 44310-3502.

Cerridwen, the Celtic Goddess of wisdom, was the muse who brought inspiration to storytellers and those in the creative arts. Cerridwen Press encompasses the best and most innovative stories in all genres of today's fiction. Visit our site and discover the newest titles by talented authors who still get inspired - much like the ancient storytellers did, once upon a time.

Cerridwen Press
www.cerridwenpress.com

Discover for yourself why readers can't get enough of the multiple award-winning publisher Ellora's Cave.

Whether you prefer e-books or paperbacks, be sure to visit EC on the web at www.ellorascave.com

for an erotic reading experience that will leave you breathless.